Whispers in Dust and Bone

Whispers

IN DUST AND BONE

Andrew Geyer

TEXAS TECH UNIVERSITY PRESS

This book is typeset in Bembo and John Handy. The paper used in this book meets the minimum requirements of ANSI/NISO Z39.48-1992 (R1997). ∞

Designed b David Timmons

Printed in the United States of America

Library of Congress Cataloging-in-Publication Data are available.

03 04 05 06 07 08 09 10 11 / 9 8 7 6 5 4 3 2 1

Texas Tech University Press
Box 41037
Lubbock, Texas 79409-1037 USA
1.800.832.4042
ttup@ttu.edu
www.ttup.ttu.edu

FOR MY MOTHER, WHO BELIEVED . . .

That something *is*, presupposes that *anything* can be.

HEIDEGGER

God is a jigsaw timer.

LAURA NYRO

Acknowledgments

Grateful acknowledgment is made to the following publications in which versions of these short stories first appeared:

Amarillo Bay: "Looking for a Miracle"
At the River's Side: "Slow Light"
Chiron Review: "Tea With Jesus"
Concho River Review: "Leslie Pictured"
Free Times: "Moonlight"
The Georgia Guardian: "Someone to Watch Over Me"
The Point: "Earline's Combustion"
Savannah Literary Journal: "Samson Four"
The South Carolina State: "Trust Jesus," "Ring Around the Moon"
South Dakota Review: "God & Son"
Southwestern American Literature: "Last Train to Machu Picchu"
Yemassee: "Flight of Doves"

I would like to thank Frank A. Geyer Jr., Monte Geyer, David Cox, Zulkifar Ghose, William Price Fox, Ellen Malphrus, Daryl Lofdahl, Luke Phillips, Christina Kotoske, Claudia Smith Brinson, W. Joe Hoppe, Jill Patterson, Jackie McLean, Judith Keeling, and Jay Jay Wiseman, without whose guidance and generous assistance this short story cycle would not exist.

I am especially grateful to the South Carolina Arts Commission and the *South Carolina State* for the South Carolina Fiction Project grants that provided me with time to write new stories, and recognition for stories already done.

ACKNOWLEDGMENTS

Contents

Whispers in Dust and Bone

Ring Around the Moon

I *sit* on a diesel cargo boat on the Amazon River somewhere between Yurimaguas and Iquitos, staring up at the ring around the moon. It's not all that impressive a moon as moons go—a little over half full and slowly on the wax. And every town on both banks dumps raw sewage into the water. But something seems to lighten the dark heavy air, make the sewage silver, the jungle jagged and black. My grandmother would say it's the ring.

I'm feeling kind of funky. I haven't showered for days. My hair is long and stringy, filled with oil and insect repellent and bodies of mosquitoes living and dead. The boat chugs downriver at a fairly brisk clip, stopping every now and then at some shantytown to pick up barefoot passengers or take on cargo. We're carrying a load of dried fish that got soaked during the five-day stop in Yurimaguas. The boat leaks when it sits still. The stench is so overwhelming that it covers almost completely the reek of the other passengers, and of the river.

The boat has three levels. It looks like a triple-decker sandwich of weather-beaten wood with the passengers pressed into the middle. The top deck is the banana deck. There are tons of them. Tons of green bananas pressing down on the deck above my head, slowly ripening. At every stop the heap gets higher, the deck creaks louder as it sags a little more. At first, every time the wood creaked I scrambled out of my hammock and got ready to jump clear, into the river. Then it occurred to me that as well as being the world's largest expanse of open sewer, the Amazon is infested with at least two-thirds of the world's piranha population. And then there are the crocodiles. What a choice for someone who grew up on a ranch in the Southwest Texas semi-desert—crushed to death by underripe bananas, or eaten alive in a toilet bowl. Even if I managed to make it to shore, I'd be in the middle of the Amazon Jungle. Alone. So I sit awake all night and study the ring around the moon.

Near the front of the middle deck is the seven-by-ten-foot plywood box that serves as the captain's cabin. The steering wheel stands directly in front of it, in a bit of open space in the prow. A fourteen-year-old Peruvian boy squats at the wheel and chain-smokes, guiding the boat around sandbars on the barked directions of the captain. I found out from one of the crew that the boy is the captain's son, that he's learning the river. The crewman went on to say that navigation on the Amazon isn't a very exact science. Then he laughed and said it isn't a science at all. The sandbars are constantly shifting. There are floating logs, and logs waiting under the water, big enough to stave in the hull. It's tougher to see them, he said, at night. Then he laughed again like it didn't matter. So I think about my grandmother as I stare up at the ring around the moon, and hope she'll watch through the captain's eyes.

Behind the cabin is the passenger area. The space is filled completely with people in hammocks slung two and three deep between the rafters and the rail. The hammocks themselves must at one time have been bright as the birds that rainbow the trees during the day. They are now stained a uniform mud-brown. The people, too, are hammock-colored. The ceiling is very low, not more than five and a half feet at the rafters. David and I spend most of our time hunched in our hammocks, or crouched on the deck. Our bodies are grime-covered backaches. We are grayer than we are brown.

Except for the engine, a tiny kitchen, and the *baño,* the lower deck is all cargo space. The *baño* is the Amazonian idea of a restroom—a wooden toilet in a closet with a hole in the bottom, and nothing but river underneath. This is the animal deck. After a couple of days on the river, the narrow stalls are jammed with goats and half-wild pigs. Between piles of dried fish, red and black chickens in wooden cages are stacked from the floor to the roof.

It's strange how a smell can take you back across years and miles to a specific instant in time. The smell of fish reminds me of Yurimaguas. For the rest of my life, the smell of fish will beam my subconscious straight back to that louse-infested but very peaceful armpit nestled in the jungles of Peru. It's a damned shame.

We slogged in on a Sunday after spending three days crossing the Amazon jungle in the back of a dump truck. It was the rainy season and the buses weren't running. The roads ran water and mud. We drove three days and nights through the rain that never stopped or started but just went on. Everything that wasn't green was gray. Gray water falling from gray sky into gray earth. Or else it was completely black. The truck was carrying rocks. Two Peruvians drove and slept, slept and drove in shifts that looked to be as dry and as comfortable as David and I were miserable and wet. We stopped only when the runoff cut the road in two, and then the four of us—it took the four of us—unloaded the rocks one by one and threw them into the water. Then we drove across the water on the rocks. The truck carries pieces of the Andes across to Yurimaguas, leaving the pieces behind as bridges for the road. In Yurimaguas, they load up with cargo and drive back. But we ran out of bridges before we ran out of jungle, and we had to hike the last five miles or so into town.

We were told at the hotel that a boat would be leaving for Iquitos on Tuesday, *"posible,"* but by Wednesday, *"seguro."* We were too busy sweating to talk much. Actually, David was sulking, I guess. He'd wanted to fly to Iquitos, but I managed to talk him into the dump truck and the boat instead. It took a lot of talking. I built the whole thing up as an adventure, but the truth was that I didn't have the money for the flight—only twenty dollars American for Peruvians, but seventy-five American for Americans—and I wasn't about to admit it, even to him.

Anyhow, Tuesday came and *"posible"* turned into *"imposible"* and *"seguro"* turned into *"posible."* But we were told that Thursday was *"seguro,"* which was good, because we were almost out of Intis. We found out about the time we were broke that we couldn't change our traveler's checks in Yurimaguas. It was the damnedest thing— straight out of a commercial on network TV. We walked into a one-room bank that had a desk instead of a counter. We told the teller we needed to change some traveler's checks into Intis and he said, *"American Express?"* When we shook our heads no, he put his feet up on the desk and said, *"no American Express, no aquí. Sólo en Iquitos."* He was serious. He even turned down the bribe.

WHISPERS IN DUST AND BONE

Thursday came and we loaded up on bottled water, paid the bill at Hostal Leo's Palace, picked up our backpacks again—filled mostly with canned food, and very heavy—and walked down to the docks a couple of hours early. We boarded the boat without a hitch, set up our hammocks, and settled in to wait. We had been assured the day before that the boat would be departing *"exactamente a las quatro."* Four came and went. Five became six. We sat and waited. At eight the captain came back and told us that the engine was broken. The boat would not depart until the next day, Friday, *"seguro"* and *"exactamente a las quatro."*

This wouldn't have been quite so bad if we hadn't spent the last of our Intis on the passage—which cost a thousand Intis each for Peruvians, but five thousand each for us—and on bottled water, of which we were still in short supply. We explained the situation to the captain. And after an hour and a half of begging, he graciously allowed us to spend a sweltering night aboard the boat with himself, his cutthroat-looking crew, and the hold-full of dried fish that was slowly soaking. He made things better by giving us breakfast and lunch. The boat did depart that afternoon, and it was not much later than six. Practically on time.

So I'm sitting here on a wooden stool staring out over the rail at the ring around the moon and thinking about my dead grandmother. It's my mother's mother I'm talking about. I haven't thought about her in a long time. I am thinking about one particular night I was spending at Bibby and Grandaddy's. My grandmother's Christian name was Vivian. There was a harelip in the family. The nickname, "Bibby," stuck. It was a warm summer night with a sheer veil of clouds in the sky, and there was a ring around the full moon.

"A ring around the moon," my grandmother said, her voice

hushed, as though she was passing on some kind of secret that moons weren't supposed to hear, "used to tell the oldtimers that the weather was about to change."

I remember listening to that and conjuring up all kinds of images of oldtimers and Indians and ringed moons, and being awed at the scope of my grandmother's knowledge. Bibby never finished high school—she dropped out to marry my Grandaddy and have a baby that she named Sally, and that died after three days—but she was wise. I've never met another human being with so much sense. She taught me all kinds of things that had mostly to do with animals and oldtimers. Things like, "cats see ghosts," or "the deer move when the shadows grow long." She also told me once that raccoons breed by rubbing noses. But I was little then, and she most likely just didn't want to own up to the real story. Anyhow, she was wise.

Far across on the starboard shore, a light bobs up and down. The engines slow. The boat glides that way. As we close in, the scene on the bank comes clearer. A man stands in a clearing, raising and lowering a sputtering torch he has just pulled from a small fire. The boat jars lightly against the bank. Around the fire sits a group which must be the man's family—a woman who looks middle-aged but is probably not more than twenty-seven, the man with the torch, and three or four kids ranging in age from around five to thirteen years. The man embraces his wife. He hugs his children. He boards the boat. The engines cough, catch, begin chugging. The fire fades in the wake of our passing.

My Grandaddy died three or four years after that night of the ring around the full moon. I guess he was really more like a substitute father than a grandfather, my own father being very busy or just not very interested. Grandaddy used to take me hunting and fishing, and he taught me how to cheat at cards. I could mark a deck by age seven, and was dealing bottoms and seconds by the time I was nine.

WHISPERS IN DUST AND BONE

I remember joking with my friends at his funeral. They were impressed that I wasn't crying. I thought it made me a man. It wasn't just at the funeral, though. I didn't cry at all after he died, not even when I was alone.

A crewman bundled in a blanket walks up and stands beside me at the rail. It's cold on the river at night, even though we're practically straddling the equator.

"*Qué hora es?*" he asks.

"*Once y media,*" I answer.

"*Gracias,*" he says. He is already walking away toward the front.

"*De nada.*"

My grandmother didn't make it a year without him. I guess she got lost. I didn't cry at her funeral either, but I didn't joke. Not even when a pallbearer stumbled, and they almost dropped the coffin in the weeds. I was at a different stage, then. Real manhood, I had learned, meant being stoic and that was about all. If you could take it, and keep quiet about it, then you were a man.

I remember the last time I cried. I was fourteen years old. I talked back to my father, and he broke my nose with one punch. It was a big fist. He was a big man. I believe he was drunk at the time. I cried for a long time and then, all of a sudden, I stopped. I remember telling my father that no matter what happened after that, I would never cry again. I also told him that if he touched me again, I would kill him. It was the first time we had touched in years.

A giant turtle lies belly-up on the deck. A crewman carried it on board at the last stop. It will be supper tomorrow night. Two little boys squat on either side of the turtle and torment it. They prod its head with sticks. They yank its legs as it waves them in the air, trying in vain to right itself. Their laughter is as innocent as the trickle of urine that runs from the front of the passenger area to the back, where David and I slung our hammocks. The urine comes from the hammock of a small baby. The hammock is of macramé, so the urine runs right through to the deck and trickles away. This is the third time today it has happened. The mother doesn't bother to mop it up. Because of the humidity, it takes a long time to dry. The two boys roll the turtle in it, until it soaks into the deck.

David sits playing blackjack with Vicki, a Peruvian girl we met on the boat. We are still too busy sweating to talk much. Vicki is on her way to Pocalpa, where she hopes to work in the business of one of her ten brothers. She only has five sisters. Vicki is short for Victoria. It means "victory." She says all her brothers and sisters have names like that. Or else they're named after saints. David and I made a bet on whether she was doing the captain. He said no, and I said yes. Yesterday afternoon a crewman moved her suitcase into the captain's cabin. Last night she wasn't in her hammock, and this morning the captain was whistling. He wouldn't look at her. Vicki was a little short on Intis, and it seems she and the captain have reached an understanding. But who knows? Anyway, I'll have to wait until we get to Iquitos to collect.

I sit staring up at the ring around the moon and thinking about my dead grandmother. Brightly shining in my mind, thoughts flow together like the river beneath the moon. The jungle is a jagged black gash in the sky of water. David and Vicki are finished with blackjack. The boys lie alone in their hammocks. The turtle lies alone on its back. For the first time in ten years I feel like crying, but my eyes are dry. I wonder if it's Bibby, or my father, or the ring around the moon. In the middle of all this water, my eyes are dry.

God & Son

The deep red stain spread into a band that brightened and widened, bloodying the mist around him. The outline of a mesquite floated in the fog like a black balloon. He shifted from boot to boot next to the combine that loomed, all arcs and angles. Smelling coffee and underneath it the rich scent of ripe maize, Eisenhauer watched the sky fade blue. Then he took a last lukewarm swallow and tossed the dregs into the wet grass.

It was almost time for God.

He walked around to the pickup, opened his toolbox and in the dimness, clanked the cool familiar shapes onto the tailgate. There was no breeze. Only Eisenhauer was moving. Eisenhauer, and the sun that edged up through the mist as though propelled by the voices of field larks. The ghost of a sun, sallow with the groundfog that lay thick across the maize. But at least it was moving. Much as he mistrusted the thought of the coming meeting, he wished God would get his ass in gear.

Eisenhauer stuck the tools into his toolbelt, strapped the belt on and climbed up onto the combine cursing the slick coat of dew that had settled onto it, cursing the layer of groundfog that blanketed the maize, cursing the screws he started to take out of the plate that covered the rotor shaft. From time to time he stopped and studied the southern sky. Finally, from his lookout ten feet above the level of the field, he saw a dust cloud kick up. God. Had to be. Sending dust boiling up off the road that led from the paved strip to the gate he'd left open, then on through the gate and along the fence. More dust than usual for God, Eisenhauer thought, as he climbed down off the combine and walked over to get his thermos out of the truck. But then, with the big weather coming up off the Gulf of Mexico and due in later that day, they were both in a bit of a rush.

"Eisenhauer!" The dust cloud swirled around him as God's shiny black pickup hissed to a stop and Eisenhauer saw God step out in a starched khaki shirt, pressed jeans, and a red International Harvester cap so fresh from the dealership the brim wasn't bent. "What the hell you gone and done to my machine?"

"Coffee?"

"You ain't got a coldbeer in your cooler?"

"Yes sir."

"*Ja?* Well, bring it out, yet! Bring out the coldbeer and tell me the trouble with this fickle son of a bitch."

God's sing-song Alsatian accent was as thick as his arms and legs, his voice deep as the Alsace soil he had sprung from. Eisenhauer opened his bright blue water cooler—a wedding gift from Ruthie, and just about the only thing on the place besides her that was new—pulled a can of beer out of the bottom, cracked it open, and offered it to God.

"That combine shits fire," Eisenhauer said.

"Humph!" God said, and stuck his head up into the back of the machine. "You mean flames shoot out the ass like it's breaking wind, yet? Or the chaff comes out like turds burning?"

Eisenhauer stuck his head in. "Like turds burning," he said. He smelled burnt maize and dust, and the beer on God's breath. "Like I told Hiram this morning in town, I figure the chaff and stalks must be clumping up in here somewhere, and getting hot."

"You figured that out, did you? All by yourself?"

Eisenhauer thought back to early that morning, blackdark early, down at Luna's Café. He recalled the smell of coffee and eggs cooking, the scrape of boots on tile, talk of the hurricane coming and the flood from the last one, and old Mrs. Luna shuffling in among the farmers and ranchers carrying steaming coffee and plates of migas and tortillas. Hiram was there. He'd explained about the combine problem, Eisenhauer had, and Hiram said it beat the hell out of him but he was sure God would take a look at it. Even Hiram called his daddy "God" when he wasn't around. Old man Albright owned the hardware store and the dry goods store; he owned vast tracts of land, a fleet of combines and trucks, the county grain elevator. And he knew just about everything there was to know about maize. About the red rotary combines they used to harvest it with, he knew everything there was. When Eisenhauer asked Hiram whether he thought God was too busy to come, Hiram laughed out loud. "You think God would miss a chance to tell the world he cured a combine that shits fire? Sunrise. You look for God then." They all laughed out loud at that, every farmer and rancher at every table drinking coffee, eating migas, and sweating the big weather on the way. They all knew what it felt like to be told by God.

"*Ja,*" God said, the air inside the combine all soot and dust and beer. "That's one hell of a heartburn you done gave it."

"Me? This thing damn near burned up my field!"

"How'd you get the fire out?"

"With a shovel I had in the back of the truck and my own two feet." Eisenhauer recalled running around stamping flames out with his boots, beating flames out with the shovel, the whole time ready to roll on the son of a bitch if he had to, to keep the expanding edge of fire away from his grain. "Ruined a good pair of boots."

"What about my machine?"

"The combine I pulled up to the house and put out with a garden hose."

"A hose? With a garden hose, yet?" Eisenhauer heard God sniff. "Red gaseous bastard."

"Gas? I don't smell—"

"Hell no!" God boomed. "Ha, ha, ha! A joke, yet. Gas! And you standing there with your head up its ass."

Eisenhauer jerked his head out of the combine and clamped his lips tight, thinking about what Ruthie had said not an hour before. "You keep your mouth shut. He may be a son of a bitch, but he's the only son of a bitch in town that can fix our machine. Remember that."

"Not indigestion," God popped his head out and said. "Constipation. What you got here is a problem with flow. Did you check your vanes, yet?"

"First thing I thought to do."

"How the hell did they look? Old? New?"

"Not new," Eisenhauer said. "Not by a long shot."

"I guess then we know what the hell is the trouble. You got another one of them coldbeers in that cooler?"

"Yes sir."

"Well come on, then! I ain't got all day."

Eisenhauer climbed the combine feeling almost steady. He could see, through the mist that had thinned some, the black patch of ground where the field had caught fire the day before, and above it, the southern sky still clear. He took the screwdriver out of his tool-belt and went back to unscrewing the coverplate.

"That maize don't look half bad," God said. "If you'd changed out them vanes like I told you, you wouldn't have no troubles now."

"I got no troubles," Eisenhauer said.

"Oh, you got troubles," God said. "Two straight years not paying out at the bank, a crop of maize so ripe it's about to sprout on the stalk, a broke-down combine, and a hurricane coming." God's eyes, over the beer can, burned into Eisenhauer. "And three payments back on that same combine, to me."

Eisenhauer mashed his teeth together until it felt like they'd explode.

"So," God said. "You got no troubles?"

"Who doesn't?" Eisenhauer ground out at last. "Who doesn't have troubles?"

"Ja, the land payments and the combine payments and the waiting to see what those bastards in Washington are going to do with the farm program, without which all the little guys that have managed to hang on all this time will go down."

Little guys, Eisenhauer thought, like me.

He dug out the last of the screws and lifted off the coverplate. Then in God went, the red International Harvester cap disappearing down into the rotor shaft, but the voice going on about lobbyists and special interests. Eisenhauer went back to scanning the sky. What would it be like, he wondered, to be one of the big guys? Buying things new with cash instead of used on credit. Not having to borrow to plant. More land, more grain in the ground, new

combines and trucks to harvest and haul it, your own grain elevator to process with. Your own hardware store.

"I can't see a damn thing. Give me a flashlight."

A hand appeared. Short, stubby fingers snapped.

Eisenhauer took the flashlight out of his toolbelt and slapped it
down into them. "Okay?"

"Crescent wrench." The hand appeared. Fingers snapped.

Eisenhauer slapped the wrench down into them. "Okay?"

"Ratchet." Snap. "Nine-sixteenths socket." Snap, snap.

Steady, Eisenhauer told himself.

"Screwdriver."

"Okay?"

"No. A straight-edge." Snap, snap, snap.

Eisenhauer tried to focus on Ruthie waiting at home, counting
on him. Counting . . . One, two, three . . .

"No! A bigger straight-edge! Eisenhauer!"

Four, five, six . . . the sky, he thought. Look at the sky.

Ping. Ping. Ping. Eisenhauer saw the hand appear again, and with
it an empty beer can that God sent bouncing down the side of the
combine into the field.

"You ain't got another coldbeer, yet?"

Seven, eight . . . Keep your mouth shut, keep your mouth shut,
keep . . . nine, nine. . . He started down off the combine.

"Jackass! Leave the toolbelt."

Ten, ten, ten. Eisenhauer hauled himself up, yanked the toolbelt
from around his waist, and banged it down next to the hole in the
machine. But as he started back down, he felt himself lose his purchase. He fell ten feet and slammed into the wet grass, feeling a burst
of pain shoot through his knees.

Out of the blue, as though it had come down out of the sky,
Eisenhauer recalled the time he and Hiram put a rat in a fifty-five-

gallon drum half-full of water, just to see how long it could swim. They started out one Friday in the Ag Shop at school, the rat swimming hard and Hiram laughing and betting it would all be over by the end of the day. But when the final bell rang, the rat was still hanging on. So they left him there all weekend long. When they came back Monday morning, the rat was still treading water. They couldn't any of them believe it. Particularly not Hiram Albright, who'd never put up with this kind of resistance from anybody but his daddy, anytime in his life. It was him that put the lid on the barrel. Eisenhauer was all for letting the rat go free. It seemed like, after three days swimming for his life, he'd more than earned it. But by now every boy in the Ag Shop was involved and they outnumbered him twenty to one. So he stood back and watched Hiram clamp that lid on tight. By the time Eisenhauer could talk them into taking the lid off again, the rat had drowned. It couldn't have been more than a half-hour later. That was the part Eisenhauer had seen so many nights since, in his dreams. The better part of three days fighting to stay afloat in that slick-sided barrel, alone with no purchase. Then after only thirty minutes in the dark, face down. Done.

It was then Eisenhauer felt the howl coming. He felt it claw its way up from deep down. He bit hard on his tongue, trying to choke it back. But the howl kept rising through him, the sound like screaming underwater. He felt it burst out his nose, out his tight-clamped lips, the world all slick metal sides and the sky turned to water. Until finally he felt the pain in his tongue start to balance out the knee-pain. And he stood up, snatched a beer out of his cooler, and turned to face the combine with its gutful of God.

"God!" he yelled. God's head popped out of the dark and he rifled the beer at it, the can spinning like a bullet in a shallow arc and Eisenhauer hoping with everything in him that it would bore clean through the back of God's skull. "Take your goddamn beer, to your goddamn truck, and get your goddamn ass out of here! Okay?"

God plucked the beer out of the air, cracked it open, eyed Eisenhauer over it. "That noise you made," God said. "Did it help?"

"You mean calling you God, or cussing you?"

"Before that. The noise. Did it help?"

"Goddamn right it helped," Eisenhauer said. "Now go on. Get your ass down to the bank and foreclose."

God slit-eyed Eisenhauer.

Eisenhauer stared back at God. He looked hard and waited, tensed up and ready for whatever might come, but God made no move. Then Eisenhauer saw what looked like a grin crease the corners of God's eyes. Sure enough. And standing there watching that grin spread in deep brown furrows across God's sun-leathered cheeks, Eisenhauer didn't know what to think.

"What? And miss my chance to tell the world I cured a combine that shits fire?"

"Now how in the hell did you know about that?"

"I hear God knows it all. And tells it all, too."

"Damn right. Whether you want to hear it or not."

"*Ja, gut!*" God banged the combine and belly-laughed. "I hear that, too. Now, back to work. Okay?"

"Okay by me." Eisenhauer felt himself actually grin back at the son of a bitch. He couldn't believe it. But if God said work, he was willing to give it a go.

Down in the guts of the combine it was cramped and dark and the stink of burnt stuff was so strong he could hardly breathe. The long narrow space they were in, the rotor shaft, stretched from the front all the way through to the back of the machine. God aimed the flashlight at one of the spots where the vanes came off the rotor, four sets of metal slats about a foot long, worn so silvery-smooth by friction they shone back the light.

"Them vanes are wore out. They don't push the grain along like they ought to. So you got stalks and grain and chaff piling up against that one-ton rotor, and all that dry stuff is getting hot enough to burn. Them vanes need replacing. I told you that when you bought the damn thing."

"Don't you think I know that?" Eisenhauer said. "What I need to find out is, will it run?"

"Oh, it'll run, yet. The trouble is how far."

"What does that mean?"

"What I done is reset them vanes to fast. You're gonna lose some grain that way, but you'll be able to go through the field quicker. So maybe the dry stuff won't build up so much against that rotor, and this big red son of a bitch won't shit fire no more. Anyways, not so much as before."

They crawled out and reset the coverplate. Then they climbed down off the machine. The sun had burned off the mist but the air was still thick with moisture and the grass all around shone with dew. Eisenhauer checked the sky. They both did. What they saw stopped them mid-stride. There on the far edge of the southern horizon was the gray smudge of clouds Eisenhauer had been scanning for since dawn.

"Damn," he said.

"*Ja*, she's sure enough coming. And she's bringing a flood."

"How long you figure before the maize is dry enough to run?"

"Eleven. Eleven-thirty, maybe."

"It's gonna to have to be earlier."

"*Ja.*" God shook his head. "I wish you luck."

Eisenhauer greased the combine and watched the gray smudge of clouds slowly spread. Around nine-thirty, he climbed into the cabin and cranked up. He pulled into the field, listening to the steady *whoosh* of blades cutting grain. The sound should've been lighter, drier. More of a hiss. He looked back from time to time for any sign of fire. When he reached the far end of the field he stopped, walked a ways out into the swath he'd cut, and checked the ground. Sure enough. There among the chaff and stalks, dark red kernels of ripe maize littered the sand.

It couldn't have been more than a couple of rounds later that he saw the grain truck. All the way across the field it looked like a kid's toy, even though it was as big as the combine. In no time at all it was close enough so he could make out the driver. Ruthie, her bright red hair pulled back into a ponytail, handling the truck as though it didn't make about a hundred of her. She stopped a little way ahead and he swung the combine around and dumped the grain bin. Then he pulled up to the start of the next round and climbed down.

"Morning," he said.

Lean, fine-featured, Ruthie looked just as doll-like standing next to the truck as she had a half-mile away. She rocked up onto her tiptoes and kissed him, the whole time looking south at the clouds.

"The radio said it made land at Corpus Christi, headed northwest," she said.

"Then it's sure enough coming all right."

"How was it with God?"

"We managed to get the combine halfway working again, but there's no time to fix it. We'll have to run it like it is."

"What about the rest of it?" Ruthie said.

"Hard to figure."

They walked to the pickup and she filled his coffee cup with cold water from the cooler. As he stood there next to Ruthie drinking the coffee-tasting water, the cooler seemed to shine like a piece of blue sky. She handed him a paper bag that smelled of the fried egg sandwiches he knew were inside it. He thought to thank her before he opened the bag.

"Not yet," she said. "First tell me what to do."

"Take the pickup and hook onto that spray rig over by the diesel tank. Fill the spray rig with water, then bring it over here and leave it hooked up to the truck. When you see the combine start to smoke, come as quick as you can and we'll wet it down. Remember to watch for the smoke. If you wait till you see fire, we're liable to lose everything we've got."

"All right," she said. "Let's go."

Eisenhauer waited for her to stow the cooler. He waited for her to shut the tailgate, and turn. Then he made his move.

"Work," she said. "Work! Work!"

She tried pushing him back, but he kept it up until she laid one on him. A punch. Then another, a solid left to the jaw. But he just kept on until she stopped punching and started kissing every bit as solid as she'd hit, the taste of her like eggs and cheese and bread. She broke free with a kind of squared-off stare and took off in the truck with the dust churning up behind her.

He started back into the field. Round followed round, up and down and back again, cutting the wheel over sharp in the turns to keep from taking out a fence with the heavy-bladed business end of the combine, munching fried egg sandwiches, trying to keep his mind off the coming storm. Dumping grain, though, was a problem. When he stopped next to the grain truck and tipped up the bin with its load of red maize, he had to look up to see what he was doing. And every time he did it seemed like his eyes wandered away into the southern sky, and worse, sought out that smudge of gray. Which set his mouth to working. "Damn, damn, damn!" And pretty soon he was yelling so loud he could hear himself even over the whine of the hydraulics. "How the hell can it move so fast?"

He tried holding the empty sandwich bag up to his face and breathing in the scent of eggs and cheese and bread—the smell of farmhouse kitchen, of Ruthie, of home. But there was no way to keep his mind off the weather. This year it was a hurricane, last year it was hail. Golf balls of ice at first, then ice baseballs finally, driving down out of the sky to smash his maize and peas, knock holes in the farmhouse roof, dent the pickup. He'd had to beg the Bank Board for enough money to get a crop in the ground this year. Not sufficient to fix the combine or the truck or the roof on the house. Just enough to get him here. In the middle of a crop of ripe maize with a hurricane coming, reaping a tinderbox with a combine that shat fire.

Ruthie had the spray rig down at the end of the field. It was getting on to noon now, the sun hot enough to dry the maize. With the air conditioner in the combine broken down like just about everything else on the place, it was like driving an oven even with the windows wide open. But at least the sound was right. That wet *whoosh* of blades had given way to a steady *hiss-crackle-hiss* like the crunch of new money. And he was starting to think maybe God had been wrong after all, and the combine would shit no fire that day— when there it was. Smoke. "Damn, damn, damn!" By the time he'd disengaged the blades, shut the combine down and climbed out of the cab, there were flames in the stubble behind him, adding smoke to the cloud pouring out the back of the machine.

He saw Ruthie hauling ass across the field, the spray rig bouncing behind her. Before she'd even stopped good he had the motor on the spray rig cranked up. Then Ruthie bailed out of the truck and laid a stream of water down on the flames, the whole time yelling, "Son of a bitch! You son of a bitch!" as though the fire could hear her. When she finished dousing the blaze in the field, he hosed down the inside of the machine, spraying water up into the back until there was no more sign of smoke.

"You're a born fireman," Eisenhauer said. "A fireman!"

"Try firewoman," she said. "Or shut your mouth and keep spraying."

"Kiss me."

"You can kiss that, if you want to," she said, and pointed away south.

It came to him, strangely, that he must've managed not to look at it for a long while. What he recalled as a smudge of clouds creeping in over the low rolling hills had grown now to fill half the sky.

"Oh Ruthie," he said. "Ruthie, we're through."

He felt his shirtfront jerked down, felt a solid pressure on his lips, and saw the gray sky blotted out by red hair. "Nobody's through until I say so," Ruthie said, once she was done kissing him. "Understand?"

"Yes ma'am."

He lined out into the maize and throttled up the engine, listening to the sweet *hiss-crackle-hiss* of blades cutting grain. Down at the far end of the field he saw Ruthie in the stubble with a tow sack, sifting maize out of the sand with her bare hands. That wasn't the kind of thing he'd promised when he went down on his knees to propose. But who was he to stop her? They needed to glean every grain in the field.

A breeze started to pick up, stirring the maize in deep red ripples that turned slowly to waves as the wind gained strength. Then the gusts started, and the uncut maize was like a body of water whipped in sheets by the coming storm. He knew it wouldn't go through the combine good, if the blades would catch it at all. And even though it felt like cutting the bloodflow to his heart, Eisenhauer forced himself to throttle down. The roar of the engine faded and over it, for the first time that day, he heard the south wind wail. But before he even had time to heave a curse at the storm coming, he saw a ball of fire shoot out the back of the combine.

The wind fanned the flames into a wall behind him, the combine smoking now like it was about to explode. He shut the engine down and bailed off the damn thing. But he had too much at stake to run away. Besides, Ruthie was already there. While he climbed up on the spray rig and got the motor cranked up, she kept the truck moving in the same direction as the fire. There was no need for words. She edged right up onto the fireline, close enough so he could feel the heat bite his skin, the smoke in his eyes like dirty fingers. Ruthie kept pace with the fire and then some, and he kept a steady stream of water on the flames until they got to the end of the fireline. Then she turned the corner and they worked back upwind, dousing flames until there was nothing left but a long black streak in the stubble, and he was using the hose to cool the combine down. Even then neither one of them spoke. Ruthie waved as she pulled away with the spray rig to wet down smolder-spots. He waved back and saw her smile.

He made round after round through the field, the wind whipping the maize and him running slower and slower as the sky lowered like a lid over his head. For the second time that day, he felt as though he was underwater. "Oh Lord," he whispered, "help me. I ain't asking to be one of the big guys, Lord. I don't aim to be no mover or shaker. All I ask is to hang on."

As if in answer, the clouds blotted out the last piece of blue sky. The wind in this life, Eisenhauer thought, blows mostly against you. But just then he saw another combine pull into the field. He saw the big red International Harvester moving toward him, cutting a swath of stubble across the windswept maize. Hiram, he thought. Had to be. Then another machine started in. God, he saw, as the combine moved closer. The impossible-to-pin-down son of a bitch was driving it himself.

Then Eisenhauer looked at Ruthie, done now with dousing

smolder-spots and back out in the stubble with a tow sack, gleaning maize out of the sand. And the fact that he was going to get his crop in, that he'd be able to fulfill his contract, that he'd make it through another year—all of it paled. Paled just to details, compared to the sight of Ruthie on her knees in the stubble, and the knowledge that tonight when the storm rolled in and the roof was leaking, enough maybe to flood the whole house, they'd be swimming together. Himself and Ruthie swimming together, there in the dark.

Trust Jesus

The son of a bitch, she thought as the connection was broken at the other end of the line. You'd think he could've made another half a block.

The call had come at around four o'clock on an August afternoon, as Clara Nell was sitting down at the kitchen table with her glass of sweet iced tea. She had just come in from patching a barbed wire fence that her cattle had knocked down the night before. It took all morning long to reset two cedar posts that had snapped off at the ground, and the better part of the afternoon to splice the broken strands of barbed wire. Her khaki work shirt clung to the sweat on her back, and a fine layer of grit covered the sunburn on her face and neck.

Clara Nell ground the receiver into her ear and listened to the click at the other end become a dial tone. She clenched the earpiece tighter, tighter—knuckles white, veins bruising the rough brown skin on the back of her hand—trying to wring some kind of meaning out of a dead piece of plastic.

"Corner of Cedar and Devine." That's what the voice had said. Long distance, all the way from Columbia, South Carolina. It had been a man's voice—deep and kind of distant, with a slow, smooth accent Clara Nell wasn't used to. It held itself back as if it wasn't willing to share the space of a telephone line. "Broad daylight," it had said. "Ran the light," it had said. "Struck by a vehicle, half a block from home."

By 4:15 she was at the Carlotta State Bank. She didn't even stop to wash her face and hands, just slammed the receiver down into its cradle and left her glass of tea standing empty and alone on the kitchen table. She walked into the bank in the same khaki work shirt and faded jeans she had worn patching the fence and drew two hundred dollars out of her savings. The son of a bitch, she thought, thumbing through her money out of habit. And three months yet till peanuts came in. When she lost track of the count for the third straight time, she turned away from the counter and walked back past the antique grandfather clock and the rubber tree plants into the seething Southwest Texas summer air.

At 6:15 she was standing on her front porch watering gardenias and watching another line of thunderstorms split and go around her. The same thing happened almost every day. Some days they came so close all she could smell was the rain. The wind whipped up dust from the fields until it drove like buckshot into the shuddering mesquites, and Clara Nell started to pray. "Jesus," she whispered. "Jesus, Jesus. . . ." But the only thing that came out of the sky was her topsoil. Every day the wind took a little more, and it hadn't rained in almost a year.

Seven forty-five found her standing at the bus depot over in Pleasantville, a round-trip ticket to Columbia, South Carolina stuffed down into a wicker basket with the rest of her essentials. By eight she was on a Greyhound Scenicruiser listening to a family of Mexicans laughing together in a language she couldn't understand.

She stared through the sunset at the brush and the drought, and watched as the plains turned to pines. The pines were always there. They suddenly gave way to fields, or to tall dingy buildings huddled in concrete, but after a while they closed in again and covered up the sky. Clara Nell looked more at the crops in the fields than she did at the trees.

She had to change buses three times. The first time was in San Antonio, where for two hours she sat and fumed, watching Mexican kids feed quarters into television sets so they could sit and stare at cartoons. They called it a layover. The same thing happened in Houston, and again in Atlanta, but the Mexicans there were black. The terminals were crowded and dirty, filled with tired-eyed people who looked to Clara Nell like a dose of hard work would do them good.

Not that the boy had been much of a worker. It came to her in a flash—like Wednesday-night visions at the Rock Harbor House of Prayer—out of the dark pines between Lake Charles and New Orleans. His father never worked him hard enough. He had it way too easy right from the start.

Neither of the men in her life had put forth any effort. Neither had been cut out to spend time on a farm, much less work one. The boy had gotten along by getting over—staying away as much as he could and slacking off when he couldn't. He'd hoe a field of peanuts eight rows at a time if Clara Nell didn't watch him close. Pull just what weeds showed over the tops of the vines and leave the rest in

WHISPERS IN DUST AND BONE

the field. Followed right in his daddy's footsteps. The old man had come in from the field one day and laid his head on the kitchen table. She knew it was over when she saw the look in his eyes. They had that empty look a bull calf's eyes get right after he's been castrated, when he figures out exactly what it is that you've got in your hands. He went through the motions for a while after that, but by harvest time he was gone.

The people in the bus terminals didn't have much to say to Clara Nell, which suited her just fine. She had nothing at all to say to them. She'd started getting angry back in Carlotta, before she'd even hung up the phone, and it built up steadily as the bus covered ground, as though the shaft that drove the tires wound some coil inside her tighter and tighter. The farther east she traveled, the madder she got, her insides twisted up so tight it seemed like something had to burst.

She didn't even say a word to the ticket-takers, just shoved her ticket into their soft city hands and glared up at them with hard eyes. She drank sodawaters out of machines and ate sandwiches out of her wicker basket. When she climbed onto the bus she took a window seat on the right side near the back, settled in like a stone, and stared out at the pines. The aisle seat next to her stayed empty the whole way.

The boy took off not long after his father left, and Clara Nell went on alone. For five years she had waited, for five years worked and prayed—watching every morning as she left the house for a familiar puff of dust on her road. Neither one of them had ever bothered.

When the bus pulled into the station at Columbia she walked out of the terminal and climbed into a taxi, sliding her wicker basket across the sliced upholstery and locking both doors. Clara Nell hunkered down into the seat of the cab as if she were expecting a siege. She handed an address to the gray-headed black man at the wheel. He pulled away from the curb.

As they drove downtown into the shadows of tall buildings, Clara Nell glared out the windows at people on the front porches of red brick houses perched on perfect lawns. She glared at people in cars and on sidewalks, and at the houses and the cars and the sidewalks themselves. But she took it all in. Trying—without knowing that she was trying—to figure out what it was that had happened to him by understanding this manicured, red-bricked place he had left her for.

Clara Nell stepped out of the cab in front of what looked like a single block of sandstone that had been torn away and carried there to be carved on and hollowed out. She slammed shut the back door and paid the fare, amazed it could cost more than ten dollars to ride in the back seat of an old yellow Ford being driven by an old black man. Forty concrete steps led up to a square dark hole in the side of the building. Slivers of glass embedded in the cement glittered in the afternoon sun. Clara Nell took the steps one at a time.

The air inside was as cold and dark as the air inside a cave. Clara Nell stopped just inside the door and waited for her eyes to adjust. A man in uniform slid gradually into focus behind a desk to the right of the door. She pulled a sheaf of papers out of her wicker basket and passed them to the man at the desk, who handed her a white slip of paper and directed her deeper into the building.

She wound her way through deserted corridors beneath banks of fluorescent lights. Plastic plants gathered dust at regular intervals along the blank white walls. The odor of strong antiseptics left a stale aftertaste on Clara Nell's tongue. The only sound besides the clack of her boot heels was the hum of machinery someplace deep inside the walls.

She found her way into a room as big as a bus terminal, with a vaulted ceiling and three long horizontal rows of square black doors on the back wall. An older man with stooped shoulders and a worn-out look walked up and asked if he could help her. He had on a white jacket, and his rubber-soled shoes squeaked on the white tile floor when he moved his feet. The voice was slow and deep, the accent familiar—it was the same voice that had traveled over a thousand miles of telephone lines to force its way into her kitchen. She clenched her teeth and handed him the slip of paper she'd gotten at the front desk. He walked over to the far wall and opened the third door from the left on the bottom row.

The blond hair she'd made him keep short had gotten long and stringy and matted with blood. What was left of the face seemed different, grown old somehow—as though five years had been a lifetime. The tan was there, but the hands looked soft, not hard and callused like they should've been. Like she remembered. Then she saw the scars—jagged white seams up the left arm all the way from the wrist to the armpit—and that coiled-up spring deep down inside twisted up until she thought her joints would lock.

"That ain't him," she wanted to say. "That ain't him." The words clawed like cats at the back of her throat, but the dead space between her and her boy drowned the life out of them.

She was drawn down the steps and through the shadows of tall buildings, following a set of scars to the corner of Cedar and Devine. She felt the excess moisture in her lungs, the air not dry like the air she was used to. The sticky heat stole what strength she had left, and made every hill she climbed feel a little higher. She came to a long, low building of blackened brick—a hollow shell that looked as if it had been burned out and left to rot. The words TRUST JESUS had been scrawled on one wall in white letters as tall as Clara Nell. She stopped beside the wall and looked up toward the letters, but the only thing she could see was her boy.

She passed out of the downtown area, through a business district filled with restaurants and bars, back into the red brick neighborhoods. The grass on the lawns was so green it hurt her eyes, but the leaves on the trees hung limp on branches that leaned away from the sun.

Half a block from home. The thought ran circles through her head as she plodded up and down the hills, the tight-wound coil unwinding bit by bit, driving her steps after what strength she had left was gone. It seemed to her he'd lived his whole life a half a block from home.

Except the scars. If there was one thing in his life he ever got right, it had to be those scars. She remembered the day he'd gotten them, dragged behind a tractor, hooked onto a roll of barbed wire by the flesh of his left arm. The three of them had been building the barbed wire fence they'd left her to patch alone. It had taken a while for the man on the tractor to figure out what was going on, and even longer before he tried to help out. But by the time his father's feet hit the ground, the boy had torn himself off the barbed wire and stood there dripping blood onto the sand. He stared into his father's eyes that were bloodshot, then pulled his gloves back on and straightened the reel of wire. The older man looked away. That had been the son she'd wanted. Not the soft long-haired thing on the slab.

Trust jesus. It was spray-painted in black letters on the narrow sidewalk that ran alongside Devine. The sight of it brought back the smell of rain that never fell and the sound of topsoil hissing into mesquites. Clara Nell stepped on the letters as she moved up the street.

The traffic light turned green, then yellow, then red, then back to green again, reflected off faded asphalt. Corner of Cedar and Devine. Clara Nell stood next to a dun-colored clothing store with a black evening gown in the window. Next door was a store that sold knickknacks behind a stucco facade the color of raw meat. An old junior high school sat back from the corner. Opposite Clara Nell stood a red brick church with a sign out front that had the words TRUST JESUS in rainbow-colored letters that glowed in the dark. A light-up plastic Savior spread His arms wide underneath it. No answers, not even a clue, just concrete and confusion and the sun going down.

Clara Nell crossed the intersection and walked toward the red brick church, moving slowly across the lawn to stand at the statue's feet. Her boots sank a little into freshly-cut grass. Jesus gleamed softly in the gathering twilight. His features were weathered by long exposure to the Southern sun, the eyes faded almost white. Clara Nell glared up past the plastic beard and the cataracts—as if demanding some explanation, some kind of answer—into eyes that looked back the way she had come. His lips were parted, the beginning evening hushed, expectant. But Jesus stared blind into the waiting pines, and was silent.

Second Coming

The norther blew in dry, blasting across the plains and kicking up the dustcloud Clara Nell had watched out her windows since noon, the sky hazy brown in the north and the sunset angry red, an omen. Dust hissed into the mesquites with the early November dark, whispering of change; the wind in the eaves howling that winter had come early. Clara Nell shut her windows tight and turned up the TV.

At ten-fifteen something big thudded into the north wall hard enough to make the whole house shudder. But the gust died. The walls settled back into silence. And Clara Nell heard the TV weatherman forecast the hard freeze that ached in her joints already enough to keep her laid up all afternoon.

That night Clara Nell dreamed she was falling from the sky. She was trying to save someone as she fell. Someone familiar. But he was sealed up in a white envelope, so she couldn't tell who. The cold of the high air numbed her fingers and there was a blizzard blowing below so that when she finally caught hold of the envelope, and fumbled to break the seal, the wind carried it away into a world of frozen white—carried them away, the envelope and the familiar someone inside it—and Clara Nell woke up alone with her fingers numb.

She turned on the TV and put on a pot of coffee. She worked up a fire from last night's coals. Then she sat on the hearth, drank cup after cup of black coffee, and let the heat unclench some of the stiffness in her bending-places while she waited for it to get light enough outside so she could survey damage. She worried most about her cattle. The wind had died in the night, which meant the freeze would be harder, crusting the troughs over with ice so her cows couldn't water and freezing the grass so they wouldn't eat.

Sure enough, following in the wake of the duster a thick white frost had settled on the mesquite limbs that littered Clara Nell's yard, the tiles that had been torn off her roof, her mounded topsoil. Frozen coastal bermuda crunched under her boots as she worked her way around to the weather side of the house. And there against the wreck of her north wall, the cottonwood her husband had planted the day Clara Nell's boy was born lay stripped of leaves and frost-coated in a pile of broken bricks and crumbled mortar. The husband himself had been spineless and her boy had been dead for ten years. But the sight of the tree lying naked in a white envelope of ice brought the weight of the past crashing back hard enough to have knocked Clara Nell to her knees if they hadn't been too stiff to bend.

By the time she pulled up to the water lot gate, dawn was break-

SECOND COMING

35

ing. Through the barbed wire fence she saw splintered mesquites and one of her creep feeders flipped upside-down. The devastation, covered with frost, glittered red in the rising sun and there among her black cows Clara Nell saw white birds. Pure white of body, with black legs and faces and a red blaze along the tops of their heads like the coxcomb on a rooster, they were the biggest birds she had ever seen. Taller than her cattle, and mixed in among them were gray sandhill cranes she hadn't seen since the spring.

She banged open the gate and the whole flock lifted off with a great whooshing of wings and the stamping hooves of startled cattle. Then came a sound like the trumpets of angels—but Clara Nell had stopped believing in angels, so she guessed the sound was more like a mix of roosters crowing and the cries of seagulls magnified a hundred times. They whirled up into deep blue on black-tipped white wings, eight feet and more wide, some of them. They circled slowly and then lined out into long vees, angling away south of the rising sun.

All save one.

The bird that hung back was not a sandhill. Gray sandhill cranes flew through every fall and spring, settling into the water lot, drinking out of her thirty-five-foot circular cattle trough, and stalking dungbeetles on stiff black legs before they moved on. This was one of the white ones, whatever in hell the white ones might be. His head was down so Clara Nell couldn't even say exactly how big.

She lost sight of him as she eased the truck in among her cows. Then she pulled on gloves, dragged the hatchet and cattle prod from behind the seat, and all thought of the bird faded into white-knuckled focus on the task at hand. She cracked a three-inch thick ring of ice from around the concrete edge of the trough with the hatchet, hauled out the clear jagged shards, then smashed up the two-inch thick sheet across the middle with the cattle prod—cracking and hooking and hauling out chunks until the whole surface of the trough was clear and she was half-soaked and her hands were numb. She had to pull off her gloves to get the truck door open, watching one cold-reddened claw with its deep blue veins and knots for knuckles work the button while the other tugged—seeing contact being made but feeling nothing, as though her hands belonged to someone else. When she climbed inside at last, and set the heat to blasting, she saw to her great surprise that the white bird was still there.

She knew then that he had something bad the matter.

He wasn't as big as the other birds, for one thing. She could see that now, even though his head was still down. Her thirsty black cattle had bunched up around the trough, leaving the water lot clear between Clara Nell and the bird. He looked scrawny. His coat was ragged, and he moved funny—lopsided someway Clara Nell couldn't find words for, but couldn't fail to recognize. She moved a little lopsided herself.

She pulled on a fresh pair of gloves once she was warm enough to feel her fingers and her hands halfway worked again. Then she hauled herself into the bed of the truck and broke up the hay bales she'd loaded yesterday morning for the freeze, keeping one eye on the pats she tossed into the hay feeder and one eye on the bird. He'd been injured, she figured. Shot maybe, or hit by a car or a plane or whatever in hell birds got hit by. His head sometimes lolled around, sometimes dangled, so he almost looked drunk. But Clara Nell had spent too many years with the spineless drunkard who'd long since made himself scarce to be taken in. Finally she made out a spot at the base of the bird's neck that looked as limp as cooked spaghetti.

That was when she knew the bird would die.

There was only one thing to do for a broken-necked animal. She pulled her 30.30 off the gun rack, levered a shell into the chamber, and walked around until her line of fire was clear of cows. Then she leveled the rifle, took careful aim at the spot where the neck joined the body, nestled her finger against the trigger that was so cold it burned, tightened to squeeze—but couldn't seem to move her trigger finger. She told herself her finger had gone numb.

Clara Nell knew for a fact the best thing for the bird was to pull the trigger. Broken-necked things always died, if not right off—like the way the coroner told her had been the case with her boy—then by slowly wasting. She knew that without being able to raise his head the bird couldn't drink or eat, and of course that he couldn't fly. She knew now that he hadn't hung back, as she'd thought at first. He'd been left behind.

She looked hard through her rifle sights for a dangling snare, a blood mark from a gun, a patch bare of feathers. But Clara Nell couldn't make out any kind of a mark at all. And the longer she looked, the more the thought started to creep up on her that maybe the bird's neck wasn't broken after all. Maybe the lopsided son of a bitch still had a chance.

So she drove up to the house, took a blanket off her bed, headed back down to the water lot, and proceeded to work the bird by fits and starts into the cattle pens. Weak as he was, he tried to stab her with his beak and beat her with his wings that packed a wallop like a market-sized steer. His head flopping around on his neck made him awkward enough so that, stiff as she was, Clara Nell could mostly dodge the beak. But those wings were another matter. The bird never cried out. Neither of them did. The only sounds were the crunch of frozen grass under Clara Nell's boots, her labored breathing, the whoosh of the bird's wings as they beat the air and the dull thud she felt in her bones when the wings hit home.

She backed the bastard into a corner finally, and tossed the blanket, aiming just to cover his wings. Then somehow, maybe by the grace of God, the blanket caught the air and spread wide so his head was covered, too. But Clara Nell hadn't said a word to Jesus since Jesus killed her boy. She wasn't about to start thanking Him now.

The blanket now covering his body, she hugged the wings tight and revealed the beak. Then she checked for any kind of obstruction, but there was nothing. She wrapped a coil of blanket around his neck and uncovered the bird's eyes. They were glazed. She understood that he needed water. So she dragged him back to the cattle trough, shouldering her way through the gentle black cows, then she lifted the bird's head and trickled ice-cold water down his throat. He drank greedily. She kept this up until he wouldn't take any more, then checked his eyes again and they were clear. Finally she scooped some sweetfeed out of the flipped-over creep feeder and tried to get the bird to eat, but he kept turning his head away.

She knew then helping him live was beyond her power.

But she didn't go back for her gun. Instead she wedged the bird inside the truck door she'd left open and levered the seat back, one-armed. Then she hauled herself up behind the steering wheel, worked the bird in across the seat—neck in her lap, legs on the floorboard, head out the window she had to roll down to shut the door—and with her feet barely touching the pedals she started the drive to the veterinarian over in Pleasantville.

The bird angled his head into the arctic breeze out the window like a dog enjoying the ride. People she met on the road swiveled their heads and swerved behind her as they stared back at the sight of him—of them, of Clara Nell and so much white bird his head had to hang out the window. She swiveled the mirror and stared a while at the sight herself. It was sure enough her all right. Carrying a king-sized who-in-hell-knew-what on her lap over to the damned expensive vet.

The damned expensive vet, Jim Clayton, said he knew exactly

what the bird was. "A whooping crane, of course. *Grus americana.* The tallest fowl in North America."

It came to Clara Nell, not for the first time, that she didn't much care for Dr. Jim. He was young, pushy, an outsider, and had taken over the practice of old Doc Hunter—a gentleman of her own generation who could say more in five words about what ailed a cow than Dr. Jim could say in five minutes, and who wasn't above selling Clara Nell the occasional bottle of horse liniment he knew went on her hands.

What she said was, "How in hell would you know?"

"I grew up down in Austwell," Dr. Jim said. "In Refugio County, south of Victoria, on San Antonio Bay. The whoopers winter down there in the Aransas National Wildlife Refuge, and the lifeblood of Austwell is those cranes. The birders who come to see them pay top dollar for tours. The whooping crane is an endangered species, you know. There are only 183 of them left in the wild." He looked at the bird for a long moment. "From the look of this one, I'd say there are about to be only 182."

"I believe," Clara Nell said, "this one's got too much son of a bitch in him to lay down and die."

They carried the crane into the back and laid him on the table. Then Clara Nell held him down while Dr. Jim looked him over, probing the crane's neck with gentle fingers and working his head from side to side. Finally Dr. Jim said he knew exactly what the problem was. "Limp neck," he said. "It's a fairly common disease among the sandhills and whoopers I grew up with."

"Then you can fix it," Clara Nell said. It was less a question than a command, and Dr. Jim's eyes snapped up at the sound of it.

"As a matter of fact," he said, "I believe I can. But it's going to be expensive."

"Just fix it," she said.

"All right," he said. "I believe I will." Dr. Jim mixed up some kind of concoction, sucked up enough to fill a good-sized syringe and then—over the crane's strenuous efforts to the contrary—they gave him a shot. He still never cried out. "That's all I can do," Dr. Jim said, when it was finished. "Now it's up to the crane. He'll either get well or die. You'll have to take him home and nurse him back to health."

"Me?" Clara Nell said. "You're the vet. You nurse him."

"I can't take him. That disease could spread to the other fowl that come into the clinic."

"What about my cows?"

"The disease can't be spread between fowl and cattle."

"Listen," Clara Nell said. "I'll pay for the medicine. But I don't know a thing about nursing no damned bird."

"We'll make a pact," Dr. Jim said. "A promise agreement. I'll agree to pay for the medicine. And I'll drive over to your place every couple of days or so and check his progress, free of charge, if you'll take this crane home with you right now. And agree to let a people doctor take a look at that arthritis in your hands."

"That's just the cold!" he startled her into blurting.

"Are your knees cold, too?"

"None of your goddamned business!" She was shouting now, expecting his eyes to snap up so she could stare them back down again. But he just kept looking at her hands.

"I suppose you're right," he said. "There's a government number you can call, if you'd rather. They'll take the crane. I guess maybe that's what we ought to do anyway."

"The last time I got on the phone with a government man," Clara Nell said, "he told me my boy was dead."

"I didn't know," Dr. Jim said softly. "I mean, I knew . . . I didn't know about . . . the phone. I'm—"

"I'll make that pact about the crane," Clara Nell said. "But I can't promise about the quality of my nursing. And I don't agree about the hands."

She carried the crane back home and set him up a shelter in the weaning lot. The weaning lot was the only coyote-proof enclosure on the place, but was wide open to the weather. So she wired sheets of tin up in the north corner to make a windbreak, fixed a bed of hay behind the tin, and tucked the blanket-swaddled crane like a five-foot feathered baby into the hay bower. Finally she put out a bucket of the high-pro sweetfeed Dr. Jim had recommended—even though Clara Nell argued that the crane had already refused to eat it once—and set a trough of water next to the feed.

The next morning before dawn Clara Nell was in the weaning lot watering the crane. She offered him a handful of sweetfeed, but he turned his head away like before. She tried to get him to eat again at noon, and once more right at sunset—with the same result. But when she called up Dr. Jim and told him that the sweetfeed wasn't working, Dr. Jim said for the hundredth time that the sweetfeed was exactly what the crane needed. "You'll have to force some of that sweetfeed down him," he said. "It's the only feed that will do. It's high-protein and it's got antibiotics in it, too."

As though Clara Nell couldn't read the package. As though she didn't have enough sense to draw breath. Why was it that younger men always thought they knew better than every woman who ever lived?

What she said was, "I'll give it another go."

The crane tried to fight her, weak as he was. She snugged the blanket tight around the struggling bastard's wings, got him in a headlock, and forced some of the sweetfeed onto the back of his tongue. Then she dribbled water in his mouth to wash it down with. But try as she might, she couldn't get more than just a few grains of the sweetfeed down his throat. The crane's eyes looked as glazed now as they had when she found him, and she knew he would die in the night if he didn't eat something.

So she marched up to the house, rummaged through her pantry, found a can of sardines. Then she cracked them open, carried them back down to the weaning lot, and offered a sardine to the crane. He hesitated, his eyes distant but his beak homing in on the pungent fish nestled on her palm. Then he snapped up the sardine and swallowed it whole. He ate the rest of the can that same way, one after the other, like a kid with a box of chocolates. When she checked his eyes again, they were clear.

He ate more sardines the next morning and another can at noon. In the late afternoon Dr. Jim came out and checked the crane's progress just like he'd promised. Dr. Jim said the crane looked exactly like he'd expected. "Not that he's out of the woods yet, of course. But he's made amazing progress. That sweetfeed was a stroke of genius, if I say so myself. I only wonder whether it was the protein or the antibiotics that turned the trick."

"My money's on the protein," Clara Nell said. "Unless they've started putting antibiotics in sardines."

"Sardines?" Dr. Jim said.

Clara Nell held up an empty can. "I tried to tell you he wouldn't take that sweetfeed," she said. "But you were too busy stroking your genius to listen."

Dr. Jim's eyes snapped up at that. But then she saw the corners crease into a grin. "I suppose I had that coming," he said. "I guess the best feed of all is the one they'll eat."

The crane improved daily after that, eating and drinking on his own as he gained his balance back. She fed him three times a day. Mornings and evenings she stopped on her way back from driving through the cattle. The noon stop she made just for the crane. He took to running to meet her with his head bobbing up and down, reaching over the fence to snatch the sardines from her hand as fast as she could pull them from the can.

The crane had what Dr. Jim liked to call an equal and opposite reaction when he saw the vet. Clara Nell liked to call it running like hell. Dr. Jim came every third day and examined the crane. He said he was particularly pleased when the crane started to eat the sweet-feed like he'd predicted. And although Clara Nell never said so out loud, she had to admit to herself that the sweetfeed sped up the crane's recovery. With every examination he got harder to chase down and even harder to hold. Until finally one day Dr. Jim said the hell with all the chasing and holding and pronounced that, barring an act of God, the crane would live to the ripe old age of twenty-five. But it remained to be seen whether he would ever fly again. Or make the piercing call that Clara Nell had come to hear some nights in her dreams.

And then one day he flew. He lifted about head-high off the ground, hovered for an instant, then folded his wings and dropped like a rock, looking as surprised as Clara Nell. But the next day he lifted off a little higher. He flew farther, day by day, but always came back to the weaning lot at feeding time, kicking up clouds of dust as he landed gracefully, and then bobbing his head for sardines.

Then came the day the crane wasn't there in the afternoon. She checked again at sunset, walked through the empty weaning lot at dusk, then spent the longest night of her life alone since she'd lost her boy. She told herself it was just a stupid damned bird, and not to worry about coyotes, or cars, or snares. But the more she strained her eyes through the dark for a glimpse of white feathers, the less able she was to deny the depth of her despair. In Clara Nell's experience, the things she cared about left and never returned. Anyway, not alive. Along toward dawn she found herself praying for the sec-

WHISPERS IN DUST AND BONE

ond time in ten years—and for a stupid damned bird at that. "Jesus," she prayed through clenched teeth, "help that stupid damned bird."

When she drove down to check the cattle in the morning, she saw the crane in the weaning lot. He was bobbing his head for sardines. "You son of a bitch," she said, leaping out of the truck almost before it stopped moving and looking him over to make sure he wasn't hurt. She cussed him up one side and down the other, and then gave him an extra can of fish. Later that morning Clara Nell climbed up into the attic, took down a dusty box that hadn't seen daylight in a decade, and strung Christmas lights around the eaves.

As the crane got better, Dr. Jim's house calls grew into visits. Sometimes he came and had coffee, and never took a look at the crane. Dr. Jim didn't seem to mind talking over the sound of the TV—and Clara Nell was surprised to find that she didn't mind listening. A couple of times she was sure she caught him looking at her hands. But he hadn't said a word about them since the day they made their pact. Then three days before Christmas, he brought her a package wrapped in red paper with a bit of green ribbon, and told her not to open it until Christmas Eve. When Clara Nell unwrapped the present less than a minute after he walked out the door, she found a bottle of the liniment she used to get from old Doc Hunter.

The next day Clara Nell went out and bought Dr. Jim a Christmas present. She bought a Christmas present for the crane. And then she had to buy a tree to set the presents under. She didn't have much in the way of decorations. But the Christmas tree with its two packages brightly wrapped by the lady at Superwalmart—one a can of fancy herring snacks and the other a plain white coffee cup with a message in the bottom—kept her such good company over the course of the next three days that the only time she turned on the TV was to catch the weather.

She had it tuned into one of the Christmas morning parades when Dr. Jim surprised her by dropping in. She told him she was genuinely glad he'd come. When she gave him his present, he opened it up and read the message—UNLIMITED FREE REFILLS— and said since his refills were unlimited he might as well take the first one now. They sat down like always at her kitchen table, and like always he started to talk over the sound of the TV. Then he looked her square in the face and said, "If I ask you a question are you going to yell at me?"

"That depends on the question," she said.

"Do we have to listen to that damned TV?"

It came to Clara Nell that she couldn't yell at Dr. Jim. He had that same look in his eyes that he always got when he examined the crane. "When I saw my boy laying there on that slab with his neck broke," she said slowly, "all that blood matted in his hair, my life became a silent movie. A black-and-white picture without any sound. I turn that TV on first thing in the morning before I put on coffee. I turn it off last thing at night before I get in bed. Voices of strangers are better than no voices at all."

"You don't have to worry about that now that I've got this coffee cup," Dr. Jim said.

"No," she said. "You do like to talk. And of course I've got the crane."

"Clara Nell," he said, "you know that come spring, the crane is going to leave."

"I know," she said. Then she got up and turned off the TV.

The crane wouldn't eat the herring snacks. But he seemed to take genuine delight in her Christmas lights. Winter passed with the crane stalking field mice in the fencelines and eating the feed Clara Nell put out. He would fly off sometimes for two or three days at a stretch, but always came back acting like he was starved. He liked to set down on her roof, in the middle of that bright circle of Christmas lights, then hop down into the yard and give Clara Nell the headbob that meant sardines.

Then came the April morning when she headed down to the water lot, glanced like always to check on the crane as she drove by his pen—and saw, instead of one white bird, the whole flock of whooping cranes. There looked to be even more of them than in the fall. The flock stretched all the way from the weaning lot through to the water lot and mixed in among them were the gray sandhill cranes that came every fall and spring.

She slipped out of the truck and eased in among them, feeling for that moment as though she belonged. As though she was just another white ghost stalking stiff-legged between black cows, seeking one of her own kind. Then they lifted off. All save one, amid the whoosh of wings and the stamp of startled cattle. Then came that sound like the trumpets of angels as they whirled on black-tipped white wings up into deep blue. Finally the last crane leapt skyward, and for the first time since Clara Nell found him on that November morning in the water lot, what seemed like a lifetime ago, he cried out.

It came to Clara Nell that the sound wasn't really like a rooster or a seagull, or even like an angel, at all. It sounded more to her like a pact he was making, a promise agreement between the two of them to carry on. Then he merged back in with the others, every one of them flying so beautiful and strong, circling so slowly, she couldn't tell which one was hers.

Samson Four

Little Johnson didn't want to get married. He'd never known anyone who had. It seemed to him everyone got shotgunned into wedlock. How many weddings had he been to—been in, for that matter—where the ink on the invitations barely had time to dry before the reception started and the gown still had to be cut big at the waist? That was the way all his friends had gone—shoved one by one into the pit of matrimony by the pressure of twin barrels at their backs. He could almost feel that cold steel nudge between his shoulder blades.

He guessed it was none of it fair to Ms. Myrtle, either. Maybe if he had told her at some point that he was seeing Manna, she might've held up a little better when she found out he was going to have to marry the girl. He looked at Ms. Myrtle slumped in her chair, all blue-haired and bug-eyed, with that fuzzy mutt clutched on her lap.

Standing there watching her just sit and stare and mumble, sort of, something about "last hopes" and "ashes in her mouth," Little Johnson couldn't figure out exactly where it was that he'd gone wrong. He had tried to spare Ms. Myrtle's feelings. Kept his seeing Manna quiet longer than seemed humanly possible in a backwater town like Carlotta. But Manna had gotten beyond impatient finally, and Mother Nature waits on no man. They had set the date for Easter Sunday, just at sunrise.

He had broken the news as gently as he could, considering the circumstances. Stood there in front of Ms. Myrtle's plush lavender recliner with his head hanging lower than the heads of any of those meek shepherds tending flocks in stained glass pastures up at the First Baptist Church. He had come prepared to reason with her. Prepared to go down on his knees if there was no way around it, to beg forgiveness and ask her blessing, along with whatever financial assistance she might offer. He'd even worked up a speech. Little Johnson wasn't much on speeches, much less the kind that you made up in advance, but Manna had forced him into it. She could make him do almost anything—she was smarter than he was. The last couple of weeks, Manna had made his life a living hell. Right now he felt like a combination of Shadrach, Meshach, and Abednego without the protection of the Angel of the Lord and with Manna up on top of the pit, fanning the flames.

Ms. Myrtle clutched Samson so tight his eyes bulged and his tongue hung out his mouth. She was floundering in a sea of lavender cushions and her grip on the dog was the only thing that kept her from going down for good. There came a throbbing in her head and she felt sure that aneurysm those high-dollar doctors had found was about to burst and put an end to it all, or else the Archangel

Gabriel would blow his trumpet, lightning would flash from east to west, and the Blessed Redeemer would return in all His glory. The dead would be raised, the Evil One cast down, and Easter Sunday would never come. After all, it was Good Friday. At the thought of it, Ms. Myrtle calmed down a bit and relaxed her grip on the dog.

That little dose of Rapture had been like a cool wet cloth on her pounding head, but it was the dog that was Ms. Myrtle's sole remaining earthly comfort. The present Samson, Samson Four, was the fourth in an almost fifty-year succession of Samsons who had been sole earthly comfort to her. She clipped him herself. Sometimes as she stroked his wiry white fur, kneading the muscles that lay underneath like soft white dough, she imagined he was *the* Samson—straight out of Judges and onto her knees. And she was Delilah, cradling his head and stroking his skin. The very idea made her shiver. She knew in her heart that the Lord would understand.

Ms. Myrtle had borne two sons and five decades of marriage duties to Mr. Earl without a single complaint and without a moment's pleasure. Even the honeymoon had been an ordeal. And what did she have to show for bearing up under the fifty-year fizzle of Mr. Earl's fleshly desires?

She spent the better part of every weekend over at the rest home in Pleasantville, watching food run through tubes into his scrawny arms and drool run down his chin. The fruits of their union were of no comfort to her. Mr. Earl's eldest was a prison guard at the state penitentiary down in Huntsville. The most precious years of her life spent raising him up in a missionary's vocation, prodigalized on a horse and a shotgun. As if that wasn't chastisement enough, Mr. Earl's youngest—who she had taught to play piano herself from the old red Baptist hymnal that still stood open on her silver music stand—had run off one day to join some New England symphony and turned gay.

WHISPERS IN DUST AND BONE

Little Johnson had been her final refuge. Ms. Myrtle would never forget the day she and Mr. Earl had brought him home from the adoption agency in San Antonio. It had been a bright day in early May and she'd been sure that little blond bundle would blossom into a fine and moral young man, a comfort and support for her old age. From the first she held his heart in an iron glove, keeping him out of Sunday school and away from the piano. She taught him to read herself from the thick leatherbound Bible that had guided her family through four generations. As soon as he could stumble his way through the "begats," she started him memorizing his verses. She prayed to God every night that she might last long enough to sit on the front pew for that first sermon she was determined it would be his destiny to deliver. And yet somehow, after eighteen years of everything she could ever have given him, he seemed to be slipping through her fingers.

Still standing there in front of the lavender recliner, Little Johnson started back through the high points of Manna's speech the minute he saw Ms. Myrtle start to stir:

1) He and Manna wouldn't need much. She could go right on doing the cooking and cleaning, she would just move her things into his bedroom.
2) He was practically out of high school, and
3) Had his job down at Albright Hardware. It was only part-time now, but old man Albright had already
4) Promised to promote him to full-time after graduation, and had even
5) Offered to start paying him minimum wage.

Now that it came right down to it, Little Johnson found himself envying those meek damned shepherds tending their meek damned flocks in stained-glass pastures. They seemed so peaceful, so content.

"We won't need much . . ." he managed, hearing his voice quaver a little as he forced the words out of his mouth. He saw Ms. Myrtle pick up the set of shears that she kept on the end table next to her recliner, and start clipping the dog.

"I, well . . . I'm practically out of high school. . . ." He heard the snipping of the shears start to accelerate. With every cut Ms. Myrtle made, he saw the look on her wrinkled, rouged, old woman's face grow a little more grim.

"Job . . . ," he tried, "full-time . . . Albright Hardware. . . ." The snip of the shears rang in his ears like a jackhammer. Gouts of fur fell in white fluffy mounds on the lavender cushions. He saw Samson Four, fuzzy mutt that he was, start to whimper and squirm.

"Old man Albright . . . ," he heard himself say, "graduation, minimum wage. . . ." It was as though Little Johnson could see in through Ms. Myrtle's mind's eye. It was himself he saw inside there, squirming and whining on the old woman's lap; his own hair he watched fall in mounds onto the cushions. There was no use at all in him talking. He saw her press a little harder on the shears.

There was no use at all in any of it. Ms. Myrtle had worked her way from a dead faint into a fit of hysterics. She jumped up out of her recliner and rushed around the room, slinging the dog like a dirty dishrag. Little Johnson saw the eyes roll in her head. He watched her chin work. He would've sworn that she was speaking in tongues, if he hadn't caught bits and pieces of something about "mixed marriages" and "abominations" and "a slap in the face of God Almighty."

Ms. Myrtle set the dog down, snatched the big black family Bible off the piano and flipped it open on the bench, thumbing through the pages like a buzz-saw. She must have pored over every book from around Leviticus to at least Acts, or the Letters to the Romans, before the urge to pray finally got to be too much for

WHISPERS IN DUST AND BONE

her. She snapped the Bible shut, then reached up and yanked Little Johnson down beside her. At first she just kind of prayed over him, telling the Lord all about how he had sinned and how low he must have sunk in His eyes, seeing as how Manna was a Mexican and all, not to mention her being Catholic. Then she started in on Little Johnson to offer up his sins to God and beg forgiveness.

"Fall on your face," she said. "Fall on your face at the feet of the Lord! Fall! Fall!"

Little Johnson knelt there by Ms. Myrtle and did his best to repent, but he couldn't work himself up to it. The problem, as far as he could see, wasn't so much marrying a Mexican as it was just getting married at all. He must have memorized at least three hundred Bible verses, and had never come across a single reference to the mixing of the races—except for one or two aimed at the Jews, and he was Baptist. So was Ms. Myrtle. And so was God, as far as Little Johnson knew.

"It ain't no sin," he said in a loud voice.

"What?"

"I said it ain't no sin."

"Isn't," she said. "Isn't no sin. What isn't?"

"Marriage isn't," he said. "Now all that other part. The lusting and the fornicating and all. That was wrong. But me and Manna getting married, there isn't no sin in that."

"But she's not like you and me," Ms. Myrtle said at last. "She's not our kind."

"It don't make no difference what kind she is. I still got to marry her."

"I'll do myself an injury!" she yelled. When she let go of his arm to latch back onto Samson, Little Johnson seized the opportunity to bolt for the door. "It's her or me! Her or me!" He left her kneeling with the dog next to the piano bench.

Ms. Myrtle knelt on the floor holding Samson Four and feeling like John the Baptist. But her thoughts got all confused and she kept seeing Little Johnson as King Herod and Manna as the wicked flesh-pot Salome, tempting him into cutting off her head.

She got up off the floor and wandered around the house, five decades of married life spread out before her like the arid Southwest Texas plains. She saw Mr. Earl, in the space of fifty years, go from mediocrity to imbecility. He was better off in a coma. She saw the birth of her sons and watched again as they grew into the fruits of manhood. They were flesh of her flesh, but rotten inside. And now it seemed like Little Johnson would follow in their footsteps, straight down into the Lake of Fire.

Like a sleepwalker, Ms. Myrtle started picking up and putting things in order. A fine residue of sin seemed to cover everything in the house like a layer of dust. She wiped off the mantelpiece and the piano, and put the Bible back into its place. She beat the pillows, refluffed the cushions, mopped an already spotless floor. She rubbed, dusted, or scrubbed every item in the house on which Manna, at any time in the past five years, might have laid her hands.

When everything had been cleansed and put back into its proper place, she carried the dog into her bedroom, took one of Mr. Earl's old cigar boxes out of the bottom of her bedroom closet, and broke into her savings. Ms. Myrtle sat and watched as her hands took the banknotes out of the box, sorted them carefully, slid the bills into envelopes, and laid the packets out in a row at the back of her vanity. Then she found herself in the garage, stuffing a black plastic tube over the tailpipe of Mr. Earl's lime green Edsel and running the other end through a back window. She started the engine and sat back in the seat stroking Samson, and visions of martyrs and heroes in chains blended together in her head as she drifted off.

As he walked out the front door into the April moonlight and the sweet smell of whitebrush in bloom, Little Johnson wasn't worried overmuch about Ms. Myrtle's threat to do herself an injury. As far back as he could remember, every time the old woman had wanted to get him to do something that she knew he didn't want to do, she'd threatened harm on herself. She told him when to go to bed and when to get up. She made him go to church with her every Sunday—noon and night—and even dragged him along to Wednesday devotionals. She made him memorize so many Bible verses he could spit back the Proverbs in chapter-sized chunks. She imposed the strictest curfews. She wouldn't let him take the car. But in the end, all Ms. Myrtle had done by keeping him at home was to throw him together with Manna.

Three or four nights a week for the past six months, Manna had spent the night in his bedroom. It had been so easy. Ms. Myrtle's sleeping habits were as regular as Mr. Earl's gold railroad watch. She was in bed every night exactly at ten o'clock. Every morning, precisely at six, she got up and put on a pot of coffee. So around ten-fifteen, once the snoring got good and started, Manna would slip out of the cramped maid's quarters at the back of the house and creep down the hall into Little Johnson's bedroom. They could spend their nights doing whatever they liked, as long as she was back in her room by five forty-five.

Little Johnson wiped his feet as he walked from the silver and shadows of the full moon in the live oak trees Mr. Earl had planted out front, into Ms. Myrtle's spotless living room. He was almost through to his bedroom before he heard something that he knew hadn't ought to be—a low throb, almost like the sound of an engine running. It came from the direction of the garage.

He cut through the hall into the shiny kitchen, through the laundry room that looked pressed and folded, through the door that led to the garage. Then he stood and watched Ms. Myrtle stare out through the windshield, wondering where on earth the old woman could be headed at two o'clock in the morning. She was too blind to drive in the dark.

He moved closer. Through the haze of smoke that filled the Edsel, he could just make out the fuzzy form of the dog wedged between Ms. Myrtle and the steering wheel. He tapped softly on the window. She didn't so much as look. He tapped again, harder. Again she didn't look. He pounded the glass so hard the car shook, but Ms. Myrtle just kept staring off into space like she didn't know him. It struck Little Johnson that the dog seemed unnaturally still. He tried the door, but it was locked. When he walked around to try the passenger door, he noticed the black plastic tube running from the tailpipe in through the back window.

Exhaust fumes poured out of the crack between the window and the doorframe, and it seemed to Little Johnson that they oozed right into his head. Everything went silvery-hazy as the full moon through live oak leaves. He remembered tearing the tube off the tailpipe. He remembered trying to force the cracked window down the rest of the way. And there was something so satisfying about the way that whitewashed ornamental yard brick had gone through that back window, he was sure it would stick in his mind all his life. The exhaust fumes that billowed out of the car when he reached through and opened the driver's side door thickened the haze in his head into a wall of solid gray. The last thing he remembered was the face of the dog, eyes open wide as the prophet Elijah's, and as full of vision.

Some time passed. The town constable appeared out of the haze against a background of lavender cushions. He was swallowed up by an empty mop bucket only to be replaced by a deputy sheriff and two men in white uniforms who kept trying to tell Little Johnson something that involved Ms. Myrtle, a death grip, and the dog.

When they started talking about breaking fingers, he guessed he must've had some kind of fit. They held him down and gave him a shot. After that a lot of people tramped in and out, and tracked up the carpet. They left the front door open wide behind them.

Little Johnson wandered aimlessly around the house. He went from the living room to the dining room to the kitchen and back, picking things up and putting them down again. He hung back a little while before going into Ms. Myrtle's bedroom. He hadn't been inside since he was five years old and had the flu.

When he finally made up his mind to go inside, everything in the room was exactly the way he remembered. He ran his fingers over the pink patchwork quilt that covered the pink canopy bed. He touched the gilt-framed black-and-white portraits on the back of the antique chest of drawers. When he got to the vanity, he reached across the combs and make-up, and ran his fingers through Ms. Myrtle's carefully-brushed blue-gray wig.

He found three envelopes lying at the back of the vanity. Two of the envelopes were addressed to his adopted brothers, with their names printed on them in a bold hand. The third envelope had a blue tag pinned onto it that read: JOHNSON. He remembered seeing it only one time before, the single time he'd been allowed in the bedroom. He remembered the feel of her hands cool against the fever, remembered the bright blue band and Ms. Myrtle puzzling his name out on it with her fingers and telling him it had been wrapped around his wrist until the day they brought him home. He remembered that he had been afraid to touch it.

He was afraid to touch it now. He opened the envelope that was addressed to his eldest brother and looked inside. It was filled with bills. Hundred-dollar bills. Too many of them to count. He picked up the second envelope, addressed to his second-oldest brother. It was also stuffed with hundreds. He didn't know how many. He went warm all over. He felt himself start to sweat. At last he picked up the envelope that had his name pinned on it. It felt lighter than the other two. He peeked inside it, feeling a little sick.

There were no bills inside. No hundreds—not even a dollar. The envelope was empty, except for a pink slip of paper with some writing on it. It read:

> The eye that mocketh at his father,
> And despiseth to obey his mother,
> The ravens of the valley shall pick it out,
> And the young vultures will eat it.

BURY ME AT SUNRISE ON EASTER SUNDAY.

The next couple of days were a whirl of wedding preparations and funeral arrangements. Problems started to crop up right off. Little Johnson was positively bent on honoring Ms. Myrtle's last wish. Manna was absolutely fixed on a sunrise wedding.

Her mother had been married at sunrise on an Easter Sunday, she said. Her grandmother had been married at sunrise on an Easter Sunday. From what Little Johnson could gather, it seemed like since Spaniards first interwed with Indians, every female in Manna's family had been married at sunrise on Easter Sunday. He spent the better part of Saturday morning trying to get Manna to put the wedding off for an hour or two. Finally, after an hour and a half of outright begging, during which Manna just sat and stared at the tracked-up floor, she looked up into his eyes and said flat out, "I'm not going to move my wedding back one minute, to go watch that hag get dropped in a hole."

All weekend long after that, the choice ran like a litany through Little Johnson's mind. "Wedding or funeral? Wedding or funeral?"

WHISPERS IN DUST AND BONE

He put off making a decision by covering both bases. He went straight from the tuxedo rental to the funeral parlor. The florist who was delivering the wreath gave him a discount on corsages and boutonnieres.

Even with all the running around Saturday afternoon and evening, Little Johnson couldn't help but think about it all. He thought about it Saturday night in his dreams. He kept seeing Ms. Myrtle perched like a praying mantis over the steering wheel of the Edsel, dog in lap. He saw Manna standing naked, smooth-brown in the glare of the moonlight on that first night she appeared in his bedroom. He saw himself at the altar, decked out like a corpse in a rented tuxedo. Beside him was some moon-faced friend or adopted relative in the same suit. A priest stood in front of him, looking pious and vindictive, watching as he slid a gold ring onto Manna's brown finger. He woke up gasping, feeling as though the air had been mashed out of him. It seemed like Sunday would never come.

The first rays of the Easter sun at last fell across the town of Carlotta. At the local cemetery, a somber group dressed in black clustered around a hole in the ground and watched as Samson and Delilah were lowered into it. Across town at the snack bar that did double duty as the office of the Justice of the Peace, a smaller group in tuxedos and lavender gowns gathered around an impatient girl dressed in white. And far away, the first streaks of Easter sunlight glinted off a lime green Edsel with a broken rear window as it sped across the plains. The coat pocket of the driver's tuxedo was stuffed with hundreds. The breeze blew through his hair. He took a long last look in the rearview mirror, and touched the bright blue nameband that was pinned onto his chest.

Last Train to Machu Picchu

I somehow missed her at the station.

I blame it on the President of Peru, Alan García, who went on radio and TV to let "his people" know that he was doubling the price of their bread. I blame it on the protest that started up in the *Plaza de Armas* in Cuzco two minutes after he finished letting them know it, and became a riot in about two minutes and a half. The bread riot hit the shopping and tourist section just as David and I walked into it, and the looting became general—bakery windows shattering, plate glass crashing on stone streets, people shouting, the red-brown cobblestones of Cuzco disappearing under the sometimes-bare feet of mothers and fathers and children carrying loaves of bread, canned food, shirts and pants on hangers, radios and TVs with the price tags still on—and then everything went gray in the smell of tear gas. There came the roar of machine-gun fire, the meat-locker thud of billyclubs breaking bones, soldiers and police beating anyone carrying anything, beating anyone taking pictures—and David bobbing up and down in the crowd snapping shot after shot as we were carried two blocks downhill into the station, where we clawed our way onto the train that was already moving, pulling out for Machu Picchu early, ahead of the mob.

I somehow missed her on the train.

Pressed tight against the other backpackers who'd managed to shove their way on and the locals who'd bribed their way into first class, and their baggage, and the hawkers—who were supposed to be barred from first-class cars but waded through yelling, *Pan dulce! Trigo tostado!*—and the smell of hot bread and fresh-roasted corn carried in wooden boxes, I caught no sight of her. I leaned out the window to breathe and was distracted by the Andes mountains passing gray and green and brown, cloud-wrapped, capped with snow. Three pale, thin Contemporary Modern dancers from New York craned their heads around David's and mine, demanding our immediate attention, our place at the window, our lungfuls of air. Until a pair of gangling Swedes with neon rucksacks proposed, very practically, that we view in turns. And while I hung sometimes head and shoulders out the window breathing deep into green river gorges, sometimes stood wedged against the wall of the car hardly breathing at all, she remained an anonymous body among bodies fighting for air.

I somehow missed her.

The train braked into Aguas Calientes and the shoving match started and my whole world closed down to the black fedora and broad shoulders of the Indian woman ahead of me. The red-and-black patterned blanket around her shoulders snugged the baby against her back, his tiny face staring into mine very dark brown and stoic. We inched forward, the black fedora bobbing with the Indian woman's slow steps I could feel in my body until we stumbled out into the open air and became separate again. The Andean sunset faded moment by moment as I made my way through the mix of mud and raw sewage that lined the tracks. Up a set of concrete steps, then up streets as steep as steps, I climbed fast toward the far Youth Hostel. Separated from David and the dancers, half-lost in the Andean evening and gasping the high air I stopped for a moment, alone. For the first time since Cuzco I thought about bare feet on cobblestones and the smell of tear gas and the sound of machine guns and clubs breaking bones and I breathed a quick prayer for those people. Then I looked back down the slope at the tourists swarming up behind me and breathed silent thanks for the parting advice of the practical Swedes as they shouldered their rucks and detrained early for the three-day hike up the Inca Trail, to catch their first sight of Machu Picchu from above.

I was thinking of God and Machu Picchu when she appeared.

Below me, the yellow gleam of the streetlamps turned the mist that had started to fall into tiny drops of urine drifting gently down onto the ramshackle stucco buildings, the passers-by. She walked into the lamplight and made the world stand still. And there was at that moment no God, no Machu Picchu, no urine-mist—only the sight of her face, pale-gold beneath gold hair. Then she passed on, winking out like eyes closed into the sound of gutters draining stone streets, the sewer-scented stillness of the Andean night.

Crushed again, this time by tourists pressing forward to get the last rooms at the last hostel in town, I was glad to be in front even if I died there. I braced both elbows against the wooden counter that had been worn smooth by elbows braced exactly as mine were now and wrote as fast as my fingers would move, racing the last of the room keys dwindling from the rack behind the front desk.

"Do you think," I heard someone say, "they will have beds enough for all of us?"

I held out finished registration forms, one each for David and myself, along with my passport and two red-and-blue-and-brown thousand-Inti notes. Then, nodding down the counter at the line of backpackers frantically filling out forms and waving Inti notes, I tried to make eye contact with the desk clerk.

"It doesn't look promising," I said.

"Then do you think you could help me? All the other hotels in town are full, except for two cots in the lobby at a rather unpleasant place called Gringo Bill's."

The lean Indian face of the desk clerk looked as desperate, almost, as the white tourist faces. But his eyes were black. Black, and with the fixed, wide-eyed stare of someone terribly rushed but trying not to look panicked, they took in my registration forms and passport. In them, I saw my two thousand-Inti notes disappear.

"Un doble?" I said.

"Sí," he said, rapid-fire. *"Dos camas. Una pila."*

"Y el baño?"

"En la sala."

"Please!" I heard the voice come again, behind me. "Please, can you help me?" I saw the clerk's eyes slide past me, off to one side of the line where the voice had come from. I saw them freeze. My eyes couldn't help but follow.

And change.

Pale skin, pale hair, eyes dark green—a kind of anti-symmetry— every part of her perfect, ground fine as a lens that takes in every single thing and turns it upside-down.

"Necesito un otro cuarto," I say, feeling myself slide more Intis toward the desk clerk.

"A double," I hear her say.

"Un doble," I say.

"No hay un otro cuarto," he says. But the Intis disappear. Another registration form seems to materialize out of the counter. I hear him go on, much lower, *"Al lado."* Next door.

Two wooden cubes appear with room numbers painted in white dots on all sides, like dice, and keys tied through holes in one corner onto leather thongs. The numbers read 3 and 5. But when I reach out to take them the clerk shakes his head.

"Necesita primera una forma," he says.

"We've got to fill out a form," I say.

"Von Kreis. German spelling. V-o-n K-r-e-i-s," she says slowly, as though she is used to dictation and giving me time to pick up the pencil and find the space on the form. "Vera. Passport number: 200218. Occupation: Student. Place of birth: Munich, Bavaria, West Germany. Current address: Judenstrasse, 8+10/210, 9604 Bamberg."

"I've got it," I say. Then, *"Muchas gracias,"* to the clerk and sliding more Intis, I take the keys.

"And you?" she says.

"And me what?"

"Well," she says, narrowing eyes as deep green as river gorges, "you know everything about me."

"Only your passport," I say.

"What about yours?"

"Hauser," I say, *"Deutsche Rechtschreibung.* H-a-u-s-e-r. John. Passport number: J304811. Occupation: Undecided. Place of birth: Jordan, Texas, U.S.A. Current address: In transit."

"You speak German, then?"

"Ein bißchen."

"Tell me, how does one come to be 'in transit?'"

"One comes to a fork in one's road and plows straight ahead."

"Well, I am glad you found the path that led here," she says, taking a key with fingers cool and smooth as high mountain water. "If not, I would be sleeping in the street. Or on one of those awful cots at Gringo Bill's."

"I was warned by two practical Swedes that if I wanted a room, to climb very fast to the farthest Youth Hostel up the mountain."

"I see no Swedes," she says.

"They decided to hike the Inca Trail."

"That is not so practical. I read in the newspaper yesterday that the bodies of two German girls were found on the Inca Trail. They had been raped and murdered. The paper said it was the Shining Path. There was hardly enough left of them to match bodies to passports."

Then she digs into her daypack, pulls out a roll of Intis, starts trying to hand them to me.

"Wait," I say. "Why not buy me dinner instead? Or better yet, let me buy you dinner."

"I have a friend," she says.

"Then it must be a girlfriend," I say, knowing no man in his right mind would send Vera off alone, after dark, in the rebel-held mountains. *"Nicht wahr?"*

"Ja," she says. "A girlfriend."

"Well I have a friend who's a boy. Why not get our friends together, and find some food? It would be safer."

Call it inspiration.

Looking into her face I feel again as though I am in the bread riot at Cuzco. Her eyes catch me up and carry me along, my feet hardly touching the floor as I shoulder our rucksacks and follow Vera, wondering where in the world she will set me down.

"The Galapagos," she says, "are a must-see," in her slight German accent and her English that is better than mine.

"Volcanoes," her friend says, "and black lava beaches, and water so clear you can see the ocean floor from the surface."

The friend's name is Heike and next to Vera she looks as plain as the corn on her plate. The rest of us ordered spicy Andean chicken and a rich bean dish flavored with red peppers and pork. But Heike ordered vegetarian. And the only non-meat offering at Café El Gato Negro in Aguas Calientes is roasted corn.

"The giant tortoises," Vera says, "are more than a hundred years old. And there are sea lions, and marine iguanas. Even equatorial penguins."

"All with no fear of humans," Heike says, "so that you can approach them in their natural habitat."

It isn't the plank walls around us, built out of the same bleached-gray wood as the table in front of us, or Heike looking up from her uneaten corn to stare at Vera sitting next to me and then back down into her corn—or even the Contemporary Modern dancers waving from one of the five other tables in the café and David going back and forth between us and them—that let me know the dinner is a disaster. Rather, it is the sight of Vera sitting next to me, staring off into space and talking about someplace she would rather be.

"How do you get there?" David says, looking across the café. At the same time less pale and more colorless than Vera, the dancers lack the spark of deep green life in her eyes. Whispering among themselves and watching David watch them, they giggle as they wave. David giggles and waves back.

"You can go by boat," Vera says, "from Guayaquil."

"And hire smaller boats," Heike says, "to take you around the islands."

"It sounds expensive," I say.

"It is much cheaper than flying," Vera says.

"How much cheaper?"

Heike looks at Vera staring out into the remembered Galapagos, then at David giggling across the café. "You may find it," she says, "less dear than the cost of this meal."

Is she jealous, I wonder? Is she warning me away? I catch the eye of the Indian woman in the corner, the same one who took our order and cooked our food. I signal for the check, holding up both hands and writing into one palm until I see her red-and-black patterned skirt start across the gray plank floor.

Then I look back at Heike, who seems to be the only one paying me any mind. "That was one of the good things about growing up on a ranch in Southwest Texas," I say. "You always knew what was what, and who was who."

But outside again, watching Vera's face flash and fade past mist-haloed streetlamps, the only thing on my mind is the bathing suits under our clothes. There is a hot spring in town, and we are headed there now, climbing away from the restaurant beside the tracks. The thought of my Intis running low, the trickle of gutters, the smell of raw sewage all seem far away with Vera walking beside me.

Call it desperation.

Seeing the heavy wrought-iron gates shut, padlocked, set into a ten-foot wall between the four of us and the hot spring, I take the wall at a run. I plant a foot halfway up and leap skyward, catching hold of the rough wooden ledge at the top. Then I pull myself onto the platform I find there. Ignoring completely the whispered objections of Heike and David about capture, police, Peruvian jails, I hunt up a long wooden pole with nailed crossbars and lower it over the wall. I only let myself think far enough ahead to steady the ladder as Vera starts to climb.

"Are you crazy?" David says.

"I am going back," Heike says.

"Go back then," I hear Vera say. "Maybe we'll see you later."

I raise the ladder behind her.

Inside it is open to the sky and mist drifts down on the path that leads to the pool. A cloud of steam hovers over the water. The light of a single bulb reflects off the surface, bleaching the steam that swirls up and the mist that drifts down gray-white as the Milky Way. The light glistens on the wet concrete around the pool so that the courtyard seems to be floored with planets and stars. There are dressing rooms on two sides with hooks on the doors to hold clothes, but Vera has no bathing suit. She lets fall her long skirt slowly, lets fall her jacket and shirt, and stands naked in the light for a moment. Then she slides, lean and lithe and clean-lined, into the water.

I slide in behind her and the feel of the pool is almost scalding after the cold mist on my skin. Roils of water glide like hot fingers across my body. We meet in the middle where the water is deepest. Our toes barely touch bottom and for the first time we go past passports, past places we'd rather be, into the gray-white space where the mist drifts down from the sky like the sweat of stars.

Later, much later, I do not know if I slept. I close my eyes but there is only Vera's face behind them, the feel of her body cooler and more smooth than the feel of the pool. I do not know if I remember our coming together there in the water, or only dream. There is no sense of time. Only waterlogged fingers and steam rising up off our skin as we pull on our clothes, whispering of Machu Picchu together in the morning, and after, the train back to Cuzco and on to Lake Titicaca.

In the morning we climb the mountain together and I know that the pool was no dream. A wide asphalt road snakes back and forth, black against the deep green mountain. We walk across it again and again, Vera and me, and Heike, up through low trees and under-brush, over outcrops of rock covered with moss, dodging busloads of tourists too lazy to make the climb. Out the windows of one bus lean David and the dancers, yelling something that gets lost in the diesel breeze. Instead of waving back, we laugh out loud at them. Anyway, Vera and I laugh. Heike looks hard at Vera and does not smile. But as we pass through the layer of clouds and into bright sunshine, even Heike has to laugh at the impracticality of it—of paying ten thousand Intis to ride a bus for a mile. I help Vera up over the stones through a gate at the top of the road finally, to catch sight of Machu Picchu from below.

Deep green Andean peaks float like islands in a sky of clear water. Gray, worn by wind, the ruins cover the flat space on top of the mountain as though they have always been there, and will always be, waiting for Vera. I look at Machu Picchu and she is all I see. Vera sitting on stones hand-cut and carried, joined together without mortar into walls that once held emperors' wives. Vera walking among rock-ribbed tiers of earth that once were fields. Vera stand-ing, her hair blown back by the wind, on smooth stones that used to be an observatory where seasons were measured by the sun and stars, and months by the moon.

Call it divination.

In the ancient lookout post at the head of the Inca Trail we stand, the three of us, and look down at Machu Picchu. Andean peaks sur-round us, the same shade as Vera's eyes. I look out into them and confess that this is the first time I have ever stood on top of a moun-tain, and Vera laughs at that—at the impracticality, she says, of not being well-traveled enough to have ever scaled a peak. I try to explain that in Southwest Texas there are no mountains, only hills, and that the rolling plains of prickly pear and mesquite were once underwater, so that sometimes in the dry white strata you find fossils of creatures who lived in the sea. But I stumble over my words and she goes on laughing—at the impracticality of it, she says, only at the impracticality.

But farther down the wall, I see Heike shake her head. "You may find," she says, "that you would have been better off on the Inca Trail, lost or in rebel hands with your practical Swedes."

Later that afternoon, standing in the mix of mud and raw sewage next to the railroad tracks, I think again of those words as I wait for Vera. I stand alone next to the passenger car we agreed to board together until the train starts to pull away. I walk beside the train as it picks up speed, looking into the restaurant where we ate dinner, looking in the windows of ramshackle buildings, walking faster, running now—until David leans out the doorway of the last second-class car on the train, catches me by my rucksack straps, and hauls me aboard.

"Are you crazy?" he yells. "You could've been killed!"

"Have you seen Vera?" I say, from the floor.

"What?"

"We were supposed to be buying second-class tickets together, for the train to Lake Titicaca."

"Jesus," David says, "why didn't you say so before? I talked to Heike. She and her friend bought first-class tickets. She said to meet them in Cuzco."

"Who said to meet them in Cuzco?" I say. "Heike or Vera?"

"Heike," he says. "No, Vera."

"Was it Heike or Vera?" I say, fighting the urge to kick David out the door.

"Heike about Vera," he says. "I think. For Christ's sake, get up off the floor. They've got chickens in here."

In a second-class corridor with the dancers and chickens and David, I watch the mountains pass outside the door and try not to think of anything at all. It is easy to ignore the dancers, who are as practical as the Swedes but in a different way. Apparently their New York academy is very prestigious, and they are too sensible to waste more than giggles on someone who never knew it existed before yesterday. But not even the sour stench of chickens in cages is enough to keep my mind off the expression on Heike's face at the Café El Gato Negro and again at the lookout post—and the awful, empty feeling that I'll be seeing it again at Cuzco when I get off the train.

It is indeed Heike's face I see, and the same expression on it. We meet in the station, in the thickest part of the crowd. But despite the brush and bustle of bodies and the mocking look in Heike's eyes, the only thing I feel is sick of laughing—sick at the thought of the three of us on the mountainside laughing together at the impracticality of paying ten thousand Intis for the bus ride to Machu Picchu, and sick at the thought of Vera laughing alone in the look-out post at the impracticality of me.

"It's just not practical!" I say, forcing myself to look away. Far up the track, the engines are being changed.

"It is completely practical," Heike says. "This is our last week in South America. Vera wants to spend it in La Paz, on the cocoa plantation of the man she met in the Galapagos."

"Why the hell didn't she tell me?"

"I tried to tell you myself, but you never listened. If anyone was impractical, it was you."

"Me?"

"It was you who queered things right from the start. You and those dancers and that mad dash up the wall. Don't you see? It was David that Vera wanted. She noticed him on the train. The one who wanted you was me."

"I don't think I know what practical means anymore."

"Practical," Heike says, "means exactly what Vera is. She can always find someone else to be impractical for her. After all, think how practical it was just now for her to send me."

So I sit far back in second class with David and the dancers and every chicken in Peru, and I think about practicality. The train pulls out of Cuzco station and out of Cuzco town and into the high mountains, and I think about Vera being what practical means. Until finally, someplace deep into the high plain that runs the length of the Andes, everything in my head clicks together—and I understand that I have to work my way up to first class.

I leave my rucksack behind with David and make my way forward, wading through Indians, tourists, hawkers, pickpockets, and animals in and out of crates. But it is the conductors that are most difficult. They won't let anyone forward without a first-class ticket, or a hefty bribe. The train is very long and at the first stop it is splitting, with the back part going on along the Altiplano toward Lake Titicaca and the front heading off through a gap in the mountains and on to La Paz. Time stretches out into wading and bribing in much the same the way the mountains stretch along the high plain. Just about the time I run through the last of my Intis, I feel the train begin to slow.

The conductor doesn't want to let me off the train. By the time my feet hit the crushed rock beside the tracks they are already uncoupling the front from the back, which must wait for new engines. I run along past car after car looking in windows. Finally, in the second first-class coach from the front, third window, I catch sight of gold hair. I reach up and knock on the glass. But sitting there in her first-class seat next to Heike, Vera shows no sign at all of having heard. She just sits and stares out past the Altiplano, past me, her deep green eyes turning the world upside down until the train starts to pull away.

It picks up speed slowly, the way old trains pick up speed. A thick black cloud behind fades long and low. Gasping in the thin air, breathing the burnt-sweet smell of diesel, I search the windswept plain for a hand out a window, a flash of gold hair. But there is nothing, not even a station, just a running-together of tracks and the back end of a train waiting on engines here where Andean peaks run like low hills, empty of Vera.

Tea With Jesus

"See Dick and Jane."

She remembered not praying for his immortal soul. She remembered pulling the blanket over his face when it was finished. She remembered bowing her head. But his was a soul that had spent every moment on earth storing up damnation enough for two eternities. She wasn't one to stint a man his due.

"Dick and Jane are on the grass."

She remembered him there at the edge of their bed, sitting. He had a boot on one foot, a worn brown boot in both worn brown hands, and the devil in both his eyes. He'd laughed, when the heart doctor said the third attack would be his last, and went right on frying the eggs in the bacon grease. He was laughing out the other side of his mouth now, she'd wager. Now it was his fat that was in the fryer.

"See Dick run. Run Dick run."

"Good," she said, snapping her ruler against the desktop. "Now the next line." They started all together.

"Mrs. Green?"

Five rows of five desks at measured intervals. Fifty eyes down on twenty-five open readers. Twenty-five mouths opened and closed in perfect unison. The green ruler a rod in her hand.

"Mrs. Green?"

Then suddenly, in all of Creation, there was only the intercom that boomed like Jehovah over her gray head. "Yes?" she said.

"Mr. Sumps would like to see you."

Another year. She could feel it creeping up on her as slow and sure as death. Seven straight years she'd tried to retire. And seven straight times she'd let the superintendent call her into that office of his, down the hall and through the nurse's station, and talk her into teaching another year. This time he had waited until the last day. Twenty-five blank faces stared up at her, waiting to see what she would do. She felt parched for her cup of tea.

"Mrs. Green?"

No sir. She wasn't about to let it happen again. Service, dedication, duty—fifty years of Dick and Jane had squeezed the words dry as used teabags. Five days out of seven, she couldn't believe she'd made it this far. On the other two days, she tried to think of nothing but God and her flowers. She was seventy-two years old. She wanted to spend what time she had left at home, over tea with Jesus.

"Mrs. Green?"

She marched out of her classroom, down the empty hall that was painted the color of spit-up—the combination of milk and spinach and bile that came from mixing six-year-old bellies and school lunches and recess in the afternoon. She stalked through the nurse's station, with its bottles of pills and the blood pressure machine, and into the superintendent's office, where she stopped just short of the desk and leaned in over the little man behind it.

"Please sit down, um, Mrs. Green," he stammered.

She glared down into the bald spot that spread like a pink shiny cancer toward the front of his head that, even when he was a boy, had reminded her of a tulip bulb. "No," she said, seeing the tic in his cheek start to twitch. The nervous habit had first appeared when he was six years old, trapped in the front row of her classroom within easy reach of the ruler.

"What I have to say, um, won't take long. Then I thought perhaps we could take a walk over to the, ah, cafetorium."

Relief shot through Mrs. Green so strong she felt her heart flutter in her chest. She felt her feet grow light, then felt the lightness spread so that she wondered for an instant if she might be having some kind of attack. It struck her that this could well be what Sumps had in mind.

"You see, Mrs. Green, the school board has planned a little, well, I suppose rather a large, um, farewell get-together for your retirement." She watched the tic leap and stop, leap and stop, as his relief at finally being rid of her won out over his disappointment that she hadn't dropped dead on the spot. It certainly hadn't been Sumps's idea to keep her around all these years. If it hadn't been for the school board, who seemed to think she could walk on water, she would've started collecting her pension seven years ago. "Your class is, ah, on their way over right now. There will be, um, a lot of people attending. Hundreds. I'm afraid they will be expecting you to, ah, to say a few words. . . ."

She had seen it coming for weeks, of course, even if she'd only realized it just now. Seen through the whole thing, from bottom to top and back to bottom again—it was only the intercom that had thrown her. And now that it was clear there wasn't going to be a cardiovascular accident, Sumps seemed determined to squash the last bit of life out of any surprises she might have left.

"... your fifty years of, ah, unflagging service. This is just our way of showing our appreciation for your, um, unfailing dedication to your duty as, ah, as an educator. The mayor himself has come down to preside over the proceedings. I suppose you'll be needing a few moments to, um, gather your thoughts—"

"I'm ready if you are," she snapped. She had to clamp the ruler behind her back to keep from bringing it down on his tulip-bulb head.

When Mrs. Green walked back into her classroom, she could hardly believe it. Open readers lay strewn across the floor. Desks were scattered. Eraser smudges covered the blackboard. She hadn't been gone fifteen minutes and things had already started to fall apart. She looked over her shoulder at the superintendent, who stared at the mess on the floor and twitched his cheek. Things were falling apart all over. She took the retirement speech she'd written seven First Grades ago from her pencil / pen / paperclip / stapler drawer, where she kept it ready. She laid her green ruler to rest on the desktop. For the first time she could remember, she left the mess behind for someone else to clean.

By the time they reached the new cafetorium, Mrs. Green had started to sweat. It was a blinding day in May, one of those late spring days in Southwest Texas that felt more like the middle of August, and the sun had long since withered the geraniums that lined the sidewalk. Mrs. Green loved geraniums. She kept a bed of them herself. Her own flowers were as bright red and unwithered as the school's were dry and dead.

The sight of the cafetorium was worse than the wasted flowers. It was unnatural—a squat abomination of snot-colored brick that was neither cafeteria nor auditorium, but something in between that was supposed to be both and turned out to be less than either. It was a microwave oven. It was a no-fault divorce. It was a shortcut in an age of shortcuts that weren't one thing or another, but something in between that would've been better off left alone. She remembered when there had been a place where you ate, and a place you assembled. She remembered when a potato took fifteen minutes to boil or an hour to bake, and what God joined together you had to prove adultery, abandonment, or mental cruelty for man to put asunder. There was no time or effort in anything anymore. Everybody she knew drank instant tea.

When Mrs. Green walked into the cafetorium, they gave her a standing ovation. The tables had been taken out, the chairs lined up in long straight rows, and a maroon banner draped across the top of the stage read: THANK YOU, MRS. GREEN in gold letters three feet tall. The people closest to the center aisle reached out to touch her as she passed, and shake her hand. A blush tingled against the rouge on her cheeks and she felt suddenly like Jesus riding into Jerusalem, but with Sumps for an ass. She leaned hard on the arm she knew it must be killing him to offer her, and allowed herself a smile.

All at once she remembered just how things had gone in Jerusalem, and glanced with quick suspicion at the stage. But all she saw was a lacquered lectern of what looked like imitation walnut with the mayor and the school board standing behind it, applauding. She felt the blush burn brighter as the sneaking suspicion that she'd just committed the sin of sacrilege grew beneath her shame at the deadly sin of pride. Then she remembered that Job had questioned the Lord outright—and the Lord responded by giving him fourteen thousand sheep, six thousand camels, a thousand yoke of oxen, a thousand she-asses, seven sons, three daughters, and a hundred and forty-four extra years of life. She wouldn't trade Sumps for the livestock, and two sons had been enough to break her heart. But a hundred and forty-four years was life enough for a lot of tea with Jesus.

She climbed up onto the stage unassisted, and the mayor of Carlotta kissed her hand. Mrs. Green had always liked Hiram Albright. Ever since that first day thirty years ago when he brought her a long-stemmed rose instead of a penny apple spit-shined with a dirty shirt, she'd known he would go places in this world. Arthur Sumps had always been an apple-bringer. At six years old, Hiram Albright had a head on his shoulders. She doubted Old Tulip Bulb sent flowers to funerals.

It was Mayor Albright that she let escort her to her chair. Superintendent Sumps started toward the podium to introduce the proceedings, but the mayor headed him off and proceeded to introduce himself. She sat center stage and listened to the mayor officially declare it "Mrs. Green Day." Then she glanced over at Sumps, who looked like he was about to pass a kidney stone, and realized with an intense satisfaction that "Mrs. Green Day" must've been Hiram's little surprise.

It made her glow inside when she heard the mayor call her "an institution." "Beautiful" made her shine even brighter. But suddenly Hiram was finished and Sumps was at the podium, the smile clenched on his face, talking service, dedication, and duty—and she found herself wishing the sun would set on "Mrs. Green Day" so she could go home and have her cup of tea.

". . . fifty years of, um, unflagging service . . ."

At tea, Jesus mostly kept to himself. She guessed that was why she enjoyed their teas so much—that and the fact that Jesus was the one man who ever lived that was worthy of her love. He was such a good listener. Mrs. Green had never liked to listen so much as she loved to talk, and in all the years they'd taken tea together Jesus had never once so much as interrupted her train of thought. Sitting there at her hardwood table with a vase of fresh-cut flowers and the steam rising off the tea she brewed by hand and poured out into antique china cups, she could tell Him anything—about the strain of year after year of crayons up noses and pencils in ears, about the pains in her joints and her thinning bones, about growing old alone. She was sure, though, there wasn't a man on earth who loved the way a soapbox felt against the soles of his shoes as much as Arthur Sumps, who she realized was making the same speech in the cafetorium that he'd made in his office.

"... appreciation for her, ah, her unfailing dedication ..."

And Jesus wasn't one to worry overmuch about her teaching methods, as long as she loved her neighbor. He was as real at her table as the scent of cut flowers and the cup of tea He never touched. He remained with her after she put the tea things away, through the long sleepless nights that came and came. But in all her years in the classroom, she'd never once felt him look over her shoulder. Arthur Sumps, on the other hand, was forever trying to administrate his way into her classroom where—even if he was school superintendent—his administration didn't belong. She knew he listened in on her over the intercom. When the men in the state legislature had outlawed corporal punishment in the classroom, she'd gone right on instilling discipline in young minds the only way she knew how—by paddling them on the open palm with her ruler. Sumps, though, whom a few slaps on the palm had turned into a cheek-twitcher, a tattler, a fanatic administrator, hadn't so much jumped on the no-paddle bandwagon as gotten behind it and shoved with both hands.

"... her duty as, um, as an educator ..."

He'd walked into her classroom and said that being slapped with a ruler was a trauma, that being slapped with a ruler in public stunted young minds, and that future public punishment would

WHISPERS IN DUST AND BONE

result in her dismissal. She could tell by his eyes, and by the way his tic never once twitched, that this was a moment he'd been waiting for since he was six years old. So from that moment on she'd taken the young minds behind the blackboard, into the little room where she kept their toys—and gone right on paddling them on the open palm with her ruler. New rules had come into effect over the years, one by one. And one by one, she'd ignored them.

Gifts. Superintendent Sumps called her up to the podium finally, and when everybody got done standing and clapping, they started giving her gifts. Hiram Albright gave her a rosebush for her front yard. She got a gold railroad watch from the school board. She got music books for teaching piano to children from the teachers. She'd never played piano a day in her life. Sumps left her standing there alone, finally, to say her piece. But she was so busy wondering why she'd chosen this godforsaken job, in this semi-desert place—much less worked it fifty years—that she couldn't get the speech out of her pocket, much less her mouth.

It wasn't until she was alone at the podium that she looked out over the cafetorium and was almost crushed with disappointment at the size of the crowd. There were so many of them—three genera-tions worth of bellyaches and tears and runny noses—and after all of it, she doubted if a third of them could do much more than scratch their scrawl. All the best ones, the couple of dozen or so real suc-cesses, had shaken the dust of Carlotta off their feet and if they ever looked back, it was only at Christmas.

Both her sons had settled like dregs. She saw them down front, in the middle of the cluster of family that had turned out for the occa-sion. At least one or two of the grandchildren had managed to be absent. She remembered the last time they were all together. It was the day before Christmas and she'd shocked them all by informing them that she was rewriting her will, and they should go through the house and pick out whatever they wanted her to leave them. Then she sat down at the table, inhaled the sweet scent of fresh-cut geraniums, and poured out two cups of tea. Of course it had been a test. If even one of them had told her it wasn't her things he was after, that it was she he loved and not her bankbook, she would've left him everything. And after forty years of wedlock with a man worried more about pinching his pennies than saving his soul, she had plenty to leave. She sat and had tea with Jesus while the adults bickered over which of her valuables were going to be theirs, and the grandchildren, who never paid her much mind anyway, talked about how insects are more developed socially than human beings. She'd tried to love her sons and do her duty by them, but they made it so hard. Her eldest had been married six times and divorced six times, the last attempt going belly-up before the dust had time to settle on the furniture. Her youngest had been divorced only once, but was as godless as his father—who'd spent his whole life claiming to be the master of his fate, but hadn't even managed to die with both boots on. It was a miracle they'd managed to produce the pack of grandchildren that had laughed behind her back since they were born. It was she that would laugh best, though. Everything she had that the church wasn't getting, she was leaving to Planned Parenthood.

"Ahem," she said, and pulled the microphone closer. She took a long look at her family and at the crowd gathered behind them, their stares every bit as blank as the first time they opened their readers. "Ahem." She decided to leave the speech in her pocket. It was full of things like service, dedication, and duty—and anyway, she'd left her reading glasses in her desk.

"I've taught five decades," she said. "From the pines of East Texas to the banks of the Rio Grande. But for the life of me, I can't say why." Thoughts of Job and years got all tangled up with the thought of how she'd managed to put up with all she'd had to put up with the past fifty years, and for the first time in half a century, she wondered if her cup of tea would be enough. "I'm tired."

The audience sat quiet in their seats for a while, waiting to see if she was through. But she hardly noticed. She hardly noticed when they started standing and clapping. All at once her family was there, crowding around her on the stage, but she was ready to go. Jesus, she'd do anything to leave. The only thing she wanted was her cup of tea.

Slow Light

He was almost there. It was all warmth behind and around him, and he could almost see the light of his dream unfold slow as spring thunderheads over the low rolling hills, almost feel the dream against his skin clear and warm as noon rain. But then he felt cold air gust into his warm place under the covers. There came the heavy clamber of the woman into the bed beside him, and cold feet sought to slide between his legs.

"Old woman!" he said. "How can those feet be so cold?"

He jerked his legs away from her feet a little, right up on the edge of the warm spot he'd hollowed out on his half of the bed. He lay on his side, almost still, gathering the darkness around him like cool feather pillows. Then he started the slow roll over onto his stomach and reached with all the wore-out that was in him for the light of his dream.

"They're fat."

He heard the words come faint and far away, as though spoken across a wide open field of green. He felt the warm spot spread out in front of him now and rolled slowly onto the leading edge of it, into the sleepy feel that lay waiting just ahead. But he was aware of the woman moving behind him. The moist feel of her skin and the smell of her cold cream kept pace with him. Her feet, cold as plow blades in winter, dug their way in between his legs.

"They're frozen!" he said.

"They're fat. They look swollen. And the veins all stick out."

"They're feet!" he said, rolling slowly. "And if there was any fat on them at all they wouldn't be so cold!" But he knew it was over now, for sleep. She had gotten him talking.

He groaned as he flopped over onto the sore spot in his back and propped the pillows against the headboard. Then he reached into the nightstand drawer and lit one of his hair-tearing cigarettes, feeling the body of the woman go stiff beside him.

"Joe?" she said. "You promised you wouldn't."

He lay back with his eyes closed and the ashtray on his chest and drew unfiltered smoke until he felt the urge to tear out what little scalp-cover he had left pass through him. When he opened his eyes he could see the moon. It was a bright white Christmas moon, the first full moon of the new winter. And even though the weatherman said there hadn't been a full moon on Christmas Eve since 1950, the sight was as familiar as the feel of the old woman's feet against his skin. He had grown to know this moon, to feel the meaning of it. It meant that hay would have to be fed every morning at first light, after the sheet ice had been broken off the troughs so the horses and cattle could drink. It meant the earth in the fallow fields would have to be turned over to soak up the January rains. It meant the joint-ache and the heavy all-alone feeling of too much work to be done and too few hands to help with the doing.

"Well," he said finally, almost too tired to blow smoke, "it's just one of those things."

"One of what things?"

"A special occasion."

The quiet drew out as the old woman weighed the two things on the set of scales she seemed to carry around in her head. On one side there was the heavy cost of the heart doctor, the medicine, the chance that he might, as his father had done before him, drop dead one cold winter morning among the cattle and hay. But on the other side, he knew, and he smiled up into the moon knowing it, there was having her one and only boy home on Christmas Eve.

"It is special," she said. "What with Joey here, and Elizabeth, and a grandbaby on the way."

"Yes it is," he said, feeling the scales tip his way.

"But you know, even with the baby coming, Elizabeth's feet aren't fat. Skinniest feet on a woman I ever saw carry to term. Your feet are supposed to swell! I remember when I was carrying Joey, mine swoll up over a size and a half."

"Yes," he said, remembering her young and huge with Joey, and about her feet. He remembered the promise of it—of the three of them together. But they hadn't gotten many advantages. And what advantages there had been they'd mostly passed on to Joey. "I remember."

"It's his fault," she said.

"What's whose fault?" he said. For a minute it seemed like she'd been thinking his thoughts. He recalled his mother and father doing that, back when they'd been living. Way back. Good God, what a long way back they had been.

"The owner of that donut place next to the airport," she said. "It was evil of him to lure us in that way."

Out the window over his head the moon was so bright now you couldn't see stars. But he was thinking about another moon, a spring moon a long time ago. Back before Joey, on that first night he and the woman had been together. Really together, there in the bed of his daddy's beat-up old Ford with her skin soft and white in the moonlight as the flower nestled between her breasts. And the only thing she had on was that white carnation. Christmas moon, Christmas moon, he thought, brighter than a brass spittoon. And the outlines of the Christmas lights black against it.

"I said," he heard her say, "it was evil to lure us in that way."

"It was nothing evil," he said. "Just a special occasion."

They were dark now, the lights, cut sharp against the whiteness of the moon. But when the four of them had come back from the airport, rolling over the last low hill before the home hill on the long road from San Antonio, you could see them for miles. You couldn't make out the house yet, but you could see the lights shining out in a circle of red and green around the eaves, and see the white lights flashing on the tree through the big living room window. And even though there wasn't so much under the tree this year, and he had all the hard winter work ahead, he was glad Christmas Eve had finally come.

"Sick," she said. "Just sick. What with that big green and red and white sign, and that dirty easy drive-through."

"They might as well have hooked a tow-rig onto you," he said, "and dragged you in there."

"You could've stopped me."

"It would've been like the earth trying to hold back the plow."

"Now you're making fun of me."

"Eighty miles there to that airport," he said. "And eighty miles back home again. There wasn't any stopping you eating those donuts."

"No," she said. "I don't guess so. But now Joey is home, and Elizabeth. And they're pregnant! Wouldn't it be something if she could have the baby here, Joe? And on Christmas! Then I wouldn't have to stand on that scale tomorrow and look down between my fat feet at that dial. But it won't happen. Elizabeth is nowhere near close enough to term."

"No," he said. "If she was, they couldn't have come."

He heard her start in again on that time, so far back in time, when it had been her that was carrying to term. Then she started talking again about Elizabeth's feet and he felt himself drift—just drew in smoke and made noises in all the right places and let her run on down and unwind.

Looking up at the moon rising high in the window now he thought again about the dream, remembering the feel of April light against his skin. He knew it wasn't March because there was no chill in the air and the wind was calm and the light came so clear and slow it seemed to flow from the sun like water. You could see the light run down the sky, but it wasn't crazy or scary or like anything in the world. It was the most beautiful thing he had ever seen. Slow light of spring that soothed the winter ache out of your bones and rubbed your skin like the strong hands of angels that never got old or tired.

He had dreamed that dream only one time all the way through. Long years ago, when he was young the way Joey was now—young and strong and just starting out. But babies come and seasons change. Sometimes he still thought about it as he went to sleep. Not just remembered it, but thought about it the way you think about a thing when you hope maybe the thinking will bring it back. Some-

times when the bed was warm and he was warm in it, and just drifting off, he tried to catch hold of the feel of April light and pull it
back. He came so close some nights, the light starting to unfold slow
as spring thunderheads and run down the sky, only to soak into the
dark place behind his eyes like January rain into fallow fields.

Moonlight

"Good night, son."

"Good night, Mother," he said. "Good night, Dad." He lay there a long time waiting for the sound his father's voice, and hearing nothing. "It's good to be home."

But this was not his bed, not his bedroom, not his home anymore. At least, though, the old woman had called him "son" and not "Joey." God, how he hated her calling him "Joey." She might as well just say "baby" and get it over with. But what could he do? How do you tell the woman who gave birth to you, and raised you up, to stop using the name she'd called you by since you were born?

He lay there feeling Elizabeth in the bed beside him, heavy with the baby. And smelling the smoke from his father's cigarette make its way across the hall, he wondered if the old woman was giving the old man hell. But listening, listening, the way he always used to listen, he heard the old familiar quiet swell out and fill the house. It seemed to him, the way it had always seemed, to grow out of the silence of his father's voice.

"Good night, son," he whispered to himself, and wondered when it was exactly that he'd started thinking of his mother by the name his father called her. Out the window over his head the moon burned the sky a black-edged blue that only crisp, clear full-moon nights in Southwest Texas can be. Cool air seemed to glide in through the window. It wasn't a breeze exactly, just enough to stir the curtains like fine white feathers in an arc of wing. They didn't have moons like that in South Carolina. Anyway, if they did you couldn't see them for the trees.

"You mean 'Good night, daughter'?" he heard.

"Excuse me?"

"The baby," Elizabeth said. "You just called our daughter-to-be a son."

"Ah." He looked down into her face that was pale in the moonlight, the nose not quite straight, the cleft in her chin a moonshadow. The cleft is the grace of the chin. Plutarch had said that. Hadn't he?

"'Ah?' What part of speech might that be, Professor?"

"It's much too dark in here for diagramming sentences. This kind of light is more suited to, say, a peep show."

"Why, Professor . . ." he heard her drawl, all slow sweet Carolina. "Your young wife and daughter-to-be are shocked."

"Shocked? Well, yes, maybe shocked. But not shod."

"Joe!" she said. "That isn't fair."

"No, you're right," he said. "'Shod' is not fair." But it had been a long day. A long week. A long month of December. First it was moving, and cleaning, and a bigger place that they could afford even less. Next came final exams. Finals to take for his own Ph.D. courses. Finals to give and grade and average in with the rest of the semester's grades for the classes he was teaching. Finals to give and grade and average in for the classes of the department head who'd decided to take off early for a Christmas conference in Rome. And the deadlines, deadlines, deadlines. Then, just at the hair-tearing end of it all, as the old man would say, Elizabeth asks the Laura favor. He didn't even like Laura. Why the hell should he help her move?

"It's not my fault I couldn't get my feet into those things. They're just too small!"

"They're boots!" he said, thinking that he didn't like any of her friends much. "It's just like I told you. You buy them a half-size too small. They hurt a little, but then they mold to your feet and there is nothing in this world any more comfortable." Social chameleons, the lot of them—changed accents and opinions, even the looks on their pasty faces, as they moved from circle to social circle. To exist is to be perceived. George Berkeley had said that. He might've known Elizabeth's friends. And known their furniture that was all wrought-iron and plastic, painted in funky pastels that rubbed off on your clothes.

"On you they're fine," she said.

"Now we're getting down to it. On me they're fine. What about on you?"

"Well," she said, "I'm not a cowboy from Texas."

"No," he said, and closed his eyes. But all he could see was an endless succession of final exams yet to be taken and given, graded, averaged; newer and bigger houses and mortgages; sons- and daughters-to-be on the way. "Neither am I. Not any more." He opened his eyes just to try and get away from it, and looked up through the window into that black-edged blue—a blue more endless than any close-eyed succession of seeing could ever be. He found himself envying the old man that sky, envying him the peace of it.

"Joe? They are lovely boots. But my feet have swollen so, with the baby coming, that they won't fit into them."

"You didn't listen to my mother," he said. "According to the old woman, who knows all, mind you, and who tells all, your feet haven't swollen up even half a size."

"She did go on about it, didn't she?"

"And on, and on, and . . ." He caught the edge of a laugh now, from beside him. Then he heard the voice come again all slow, sweet Carolina drawl.

"Joe, tell me a story."

"What kind of a story?"

"Any kind," she said. "I don't care what kind. Just think of a story, and tell it to me."

"All right," he said, and felt her snuggle in tight against him. A peace offering, he thought, on Christmas Eve. "A story. Once upon a time there was a boy and a girl who took a walk in the forest. Their names were Gransel and Hetel, and they were Siamese twins. Their limbs were twisted and they were horribly deformed. Too deformed to walk. They had to drag themselves everywhere, but at least they didn't have to rely on a trail of breadcrumbs to get them home again. They could just follow the drag marks. One day they were dragging themselves along a road in the deep dark forest, and they came upon a house they had never seen. It was made out of peanuts and pretzels and mixed bar nuts, and there was a big neon sign out front that read: BOOZE. The thirsty twins were very happy. They dragged themselves into the house and a lady gave them each a banana daiquiri."

"A lady? What kind of lady would live in a house like that?"

"Why, a witch of course. A beautiful, luscious, flawlessly lovely witch."

"You mean a fat old ugly witch."

"No, I mean a beautiful, luscious—"

"But she had a wart on her nose."

"That was no wart," he said. "It was a very small mole. More a beauty mark, really. She slipped the twins a mickey, in their next round of daiquiris, and they collapsed onto the floor unconscious. Right onto their twisted, humped backs. Then seven little guys came in and danced all around them and gave them the business. The witch gave Gransel and Hetel a little bit of the business herself, then she let the dwarves back at them. And after she had let the dwarves get good and finished she slipped those little buggers a mickey, too, into the boilermakers they were drinking. Then she put the whole bunch into the oven—dwarves, deformed twins, and all—and cooked up a seven-dwarf pie with a nice Siamese twin topping."

"She doesn't sound like a very beautiful lady to me."

"What about the story?" he said.

"Disgusting."

"Yes, but doesn't it sound familiar to you at all?"

"No," she said. Then very slowly, "And it doesn't sound . . . very nice to . . . me either. . . ."

"Ah," he said. "Ah, me. You don't remember." He recalled the first time he'd told her the story so clearly it could have been only just now, even though it had been a long time ago—back before Elizabeth was a young wife, before their son- or daughter-to-be, before the boots and the flight home for Christmas he couldn't afford. They'd been drinking daiquiris at a bar called Goatfeathers, where Christmas lights spread out white across the ceiling the whole year around, like stars. They drove home through the moon in the pines and the smell of dogwoods in bloom, and he carried her upstairs into his apartment. He remembered telling her the story and then, much later, her on top of him there in the attic he'd rented his first year at graduate school. He recalled the feel of her, of the two of them together, and just as she was reaching that moment she lifted her arms and spread them wide, the way a bird lifts and spreads its wings to catch air. The illusion had been so powerful, as she kept on reaching, reaching, that it seemed to him only the fact of his arms locked tight around her had kept her from actual flight. It was incredible. The most wonderful night of his life. He told himself that it had been a long time ago.

A long time, a long time. Looking up into the sky so deep blue and peaceful, he found himself envying the old man his age. It wasn't that he wanted to get old. He wanted to be clear. A long way past all the deadlines and pressure, able to lie back and close his eyes, feel the old familiar quiet of home close around him, and watch the first full moon of winter sail wide and white through a cloudless sky. As he lay there in the bed that was no longer his bed, hearing Elizabeth's breath come slow and even beside him, it seemed that he started to float. He felt himself float up through the window and out of his father's house on the light of the full moon. But the light seemed to have softened somehow, and slowed. The moon itself, becalmed in its sailing, stood almost still in the sky and the light flew slow and free as birds. Great white birds glided slowly around him, lifting and spreading wings of moon. There was no fear of falling, of failing, only the feel of moonlight feathers. There was no sense of time, no pressure or deadlines, only the slow settling-in of December and the light of the first full moon of winter so slow and smooth, so nearly still above the low rolling hills.

When he stirred finally in the bed, feeling Elizabeth warm

against him and the air through the window cool against his skin, there was in all the world only the two of them, and another coming, and the light of the Christmas moon. There would come a time, he knew, when he would close his eyes again and the moonlight would come like birds to carry him away into the deep blue serenity of sky. But until then, they were going to be all right. Everything, he knew, was going to be all right.

Looking for a Miracle

Eddy was down on his knees at the foot of the last shrub of the day, a pink-bloomer. Crape myrtle blossoms puffed like cotton candy above his head. He caught the steady, stale-moldy reek of the pine straw bed he could feel his knees sink into, and through the back bank of windows at the Booth place he could see the Braves taking on the Astros on the bigscreen TV in the den. The Braves had men on base—two or three, he guessed. He could see the dark curves of Beulah Booth's body against their white uniforms as she did a slow striptease in front of the screen.

"Edward?" he heard. "It's almost time. I need you to hurry up with those trees."

Trees? Cassie knew better than that. A lot of people thought crape myrtles were trees, but they were shrubs all right. If you didn't keep them trimmed just so, they looked it. Eddy, though, knew the inner secrets of flowering things—how much to fertilize and when to water, how to coax out the fattest and sweetest blooms, how to root and pot and sell the scions he was cutting now. It was more than a green thumb. It was the hand of Fate. From his grandmother's bathtub back in Carlotta all the way to Columbia, South Carolina, Fate had led him to discover the perfect blend of late afternoon light and humidity to transform every window into a two-way mirror when the sun slipped behind the pines.

"Edward?" he heard Cassie say, behind him. "Come on! It's time."

Eddy watched Beulah Booth toss a last gauzy piece of cloth away and spread herself between the outline of Bronson Booth's head and the screen. The glare of a thousand points of light threw every detail into relief—the broad circle of her hips, the dark curve of her breasts that rose and fell, the frantic waving of Bronson Booth's arms as a sharply hit ground ball shot across the infield and disappeared between Beulah's thighs. There was a moment of commotion, the brushing-aside of a body, then the screen went clear. That is, clear except for Braves runners rounding the bases and the back of Bronson Booth's head. Eddy set the last of the crape myrtle clippings into his water bucket. Then he stood up, every inch of him slow and natural, and eased his way across the back yard.

"Nothing?" Cassie said.

"Not a thing," he said, and heard Cassie sigh.

"Poor Beulah."

Cassie stood on the porch in a thin summer dress, Eddy's favorite, the same blue-purple shade as the wisteria that hung all around her, a little past peak but still heavy with blossoms in bunches like grapes. He stepped up into the gingerbread–blueberry pancake scent of Cassie's favorite flower and set the bucket of clippings down next to her blue-purple painted toenails.

"Come here," he said.

"Edward, you're sweaty!"

"We could use a bath."

"You have a job to do," Cassie said. She fended him off as he reached for her, and shoved him off the porch. "You promised you'd make peace."

Eddy dragged himself around to the front of the house, walked past the pickup he ran his landscaping operation out of—a pine-colored old Ford with dents in all the right places and his GREEN LANDSCAPING AND LAWN logo painted hot pink on both doors—and approached Cassie's convertible gingerly. It was one of those red import jobs, the kind with too many gears that rode too low to the ground so it felt like you were forever looking up out of a hole. He stepped over the monkey grass he'd planted along Cassie's driveway and climbed in with a sinking feeling that had less to do with the car than the job at hand. As he backed out of the drive, Eddy tried to keep his mind on the monkey grass. A tough bastard plant, that. Not spectacular to look at, but it could take getting stepped on or run over, and if you pruned it right, it would explode in tiny blue flowers that were so delicate coming from something so hard-assed they were hard to believe.

He drove out of Kilbourne Heights, an uneasy mix of old and new money where the houses were big and the yards even bigger. Custom-landscaped, most of them. But none of them by Eddy. Where Eddy favored flowering shrubs and sculptured flowerbeds, the Heights ran more toward broad sweeps of lawn, magnolias, and towering elms. You couldn't see the windows for the trees. Cassie's place was the sole exception, and Eddy had done it all for free—the wisteria arbor, the monkey grass, the crape myrtle hedge, the patch of fancy tulips, even the multilevel bed of hybrid tiger lilies that dropped in burnt-orange-and-black swaths from the front walk to the curb. It had been a labor of love, a living wedding band of blooms woven to capture Cassie's heart. Five successive springs he'd led her out into the full flower of his creation, knelt, and proposed—only to be refused because of the single seed Cassie had sown. If he couldn't strike some kind of truce with Cassie's son, Charles, all those seasons of slow growth would come to an end today.

He crossed Devine Street into Shandon. As opposed to the Heights, Shandon had a kind of laissez-faire feel, a broad stretch of flowering shrubs, white picket fences, and pine-tree shade. Eddy was particularly fond of the picket fences. Like spokes in the wheels of a bicycle passing, the white fence-slats became transparent when you rode by at just the right speed. A lot of the yards behind them were Eddy's. He looked into a few on his way through, checking for hedges that needed clipping, crape myrtles that needed feeding, open curtains or blinds. He had to be careful, though, in Cassie's bright red contraption. Cruising Shandon in his pine-colored pickup was like gliding through Heaven engulfed in a cloud. The only thing folks ever saw was his hot pink logo—the badge of a dedicated yardman out on patrol.

In Columbia, Eddy Green had at last discovered what was for him a perfect world. Anyway, what would be a perfect world in the absence of Cassie's boy, Charles. For the Greeks, Fate took the form of three weavers, sisters who shaped lives with the threads of their loom. For Eddy it was three teachers, and a bathtub full of fragrant suds. Eddy first felt the frothy hand of Fate when he was seven years old, growing up on a stock farm deep in the Southwest Texas brush. He'd gone along doing the same things all the other boys did—hoeing peanuts, plucking fat brown eggs out of chicken nests, feeding cows—until one night when he was sleeping over with his grandmother, Mrs. Augusta Green, who also taught him first grade. He walked into the bathroom and saw his grandmother and teacher sitting in the bathtub naked, covered in foam. The sight of soap bubbles gliding across her bare old woman's breasts sent an electric surge pulsing through places he'd hardly known were there. The lock on the bathroom door was broken, and from that moment on Eddy spent as much time as possible peeping through it at his grandmother in her hot pink tub, coated in bubble bath.

Eddy crossed out of Shandon into Rosewood, the yards shrinking down now to uncut carpet grass squares surrounded by tacky cyclone fences and BEWARE OF DOG signs. Then he wound his way to the baseball park. The coach was still hitting flies and skinners to what looked like the first string. Sure enough, there was Charles with his major league–sized glove and his authentic Braves jersey and his butt planted on the bench. Eddy cut the engine and took in the slow ebb of the afternoon. The air felt warm and steamy, and the light had the golden haze that so characterized South Carolina in summer. The mornings were heavy with moisture, the low places shrouded in fog. The mist burned off as the day went on, but the wet never left completely. It hung in the air all through the long afternoons, blending in with the shade and the setting sun until the whole world took on an ethereal quality, like the ghost of a glass of wine. It was this quality of light that made people in their homes think nobody could see in, when the houses themselves were like fishbowls.

On the far side of the fence the coach stepped onto home plate and raised the bat over his head. The kids on the field, the first-stringers, let out a cheer and charged. The kids on the bench dragged themselves up and shuffled around the plate. At the very back of the huddle Eddy caught sight of Charles, half a head taller than any of the other kids and kind of gangling the way boys are when they're almost thirteen and really starting to grow. He wasn't paying attention to a word the coach said. Instead Eddy watched him stare at the ground, then watched his gaze wander along the outfield fence where there was a line of oleanders planted that looked as dry as the grass on the field. The pep talk broke up with another cheer and the boys gathered up their caps and gloves, and ran for the cars. All except Charles. Eddy made a point of smiling real wide at the boy, once he'd dragged his ass up close enough to see it. But the kid gave him back the kind of look Eddy might've given a rootworm in one of Cassie's flowerbeds, and climbed in without a word.

"Howdy, Chuck!" Eddy said. "How was practice?"

"If you hurry, you can still kiss the bench-dent in my ass."

"If you want to be a first-stringer, you have to practice some on your own."

"Sure. I could throw the ball real high up in the air and run under it. I could pitch to myself, too."

"Maybe you and me could throw some."

"Maybe we could come out early sometime and plant a patch of pansies around home plate."

Eddy took a last look at the line of oleanders as he pulled away, and held on tight to his smile. Eddy's grandmother had kept a hedge of oleanders. He remembered spending a lot of time in her yard, learning to care for the things she planted there—a banana tree, elephant ears, a bed of red geraniums, a giant mimosa, a trellis thick with yellow roses.

"You know, Chuck?" Eddy said. "There's no shame at all in planting flowers."

"That's what you think."

"You really want to know what I think?"

Charles licked a middle finger and raised it in Eddy's direction as though he was testing the wind.

Eddy headed west into the lowering sun, fighting hard not to rip that finger off and ram it where it would never test wind again. "I watched a little bit of the Braves game earlier," he said at last.

"You did not. You don't ever watch TV."

"The last thing I saw was Braves runners rounding the bases."

"Turn it on the radio."

"What's the magic word?"

"Turn it on the radio, or I'll scream."

Eddy thought about it. The only thing the kid loved more than television was baseball on television. The kid's dad had been a baseball player, a minor-leaguer in the Braves organization, until he got killed in a brawl in some bar. The kid lived and breathed broadcast baseball and wanted to be a pro baseball announcer, and of course the team he wanted to call for was the Braves. Eddy thought some more, trying to weigh the potential side effects of having to listen to idiot announcers and meaningless statistics—and listen to the kid quote both—versus the immediate mind-numbing fallout from having to listen to the bastard scream.

"You know if Mom was here you'd turn the game on."

Eddy took a long look at the kid. "I don't see any reason to bring your mother into this."

"My mother is the reason you're here."

"Well Chuck, that's true. But there's no reason we can't at least try to get along."

"As long as we don't get along, my mother will never marry you."

About the only TV Eddy ever saw was in windows he looked through. But he remembered all of a sudden a special he'd watched with Cassie one night about lions in the wild. The program said that when a new lion took over a pride, the first thing he did was kill all the cubs of the previous head lion. It seemed to Eddy, as he reached down and tuned the radio in on the Braves, that lions knew more than people did about the way the family game ought to be played.

Eddy turned into Quirk's Dixie Quick Wash with the radio blaring Braves baseball and the kid blaring back every word. He pulled into the first of five cinderblock stalls and killed the engine, but left the game on and the kid repeating the play-by-play as he walked off to look for Buddy Quirk. Eddy found him emptying quarter boxes. Buddy looked pretty much the way he always did—short, bald, so fat the belt on the change machine about cut him in half.

"Buddy!" Eddy said.

"Hey! Eddy Green! How y'all?"

Buddy pulled a marker out of his pocket and they walked around to Cassie's car. While Eddy put the top up, Buddy measured Charles's height against the marks they'd made on previous trips. Black slashes of indelible ink stretched away down the cinderblocks like the cyclone fences that ran through Rosewood, dividing all the sweetness in Eddy's life from all that galled. Eighteen black notches, eighteen car washes since he'd first looked in Cassie's bathroom window, and his war with her son had begun.

Eighteen . . . Eddy remembered eighteen. That was the year the hand of Fate had clenched into a foamy fist and sucker-punched him almost dead. It was mid-September, deep into the dog days when all you could smell was hot creosote fenceposts slow-baked in the Southwest Texas sun, and he was peeping in the bathroom window at his senior English teacher as she splashed around in the tub. She was eight months pregnant. Piled white suds slid across her belly like clouds across the harvest moon and he was standing there watching—just watching—when the town constable crept up and pistol-whipped him, and everything went black. Mrs. Fisher was scandalized, the Constable drunk. He was never sure which one of them said he was climbing in that window. By the time he regained consciousness, the sun was starting to rise over the parking lot outside the county jail. Eddy's grandmother was there. The Constable and Mrs. Green talked a long while in the coming sun. Then his grandmother walked up and dug her eyes into Eddy, deep as the roots of old oaks into places no light had ever seen. The next thing he knew there were banknotes fluttering down onto the asphalt and she spat on the ground at his feet.

Once Charles's height had been marked, Buddy opened up the soda machine and gave him a Coke. Eddy passed the kid a roll of quarters and helped him get started, then the men headed for the ice chest in the back of Buddy's truck and popped the tops on a couple of beers.

"So," Buddy said, "what's new in the Heights?"

"I still haven't made it into the neighborhood," Eddy said. "But I keep on hoping."

"Anything up with the Booths?"

"Not a thing. But Beulah keeps hoping, too. Today she did the Dance of the Veils between Bronnie's head and the TV."

"You call that nothing?"

"You asked if anything was up. Bronnie's bat hasn't left the dugout since the Braves started winning baseball games."

"What about Shandon?" Buddy said.

"You know old man Pinckney?"

"Lives in that yellow stucco job over on Ravenel?"

"That's him. He's taken to standing in the living room window at night, and loping his mule."

"Whew! Not for the fainthearted. Anything else?"

"Mrs. Dawkins bought a new nightie," Eddy said. "A black lacy peek-a-boo."

"You mean Widow Dawkins? The fat one?"

"A three-hundred-pound bag of pancake batter with body hair. Wears the nightie to water begonias, out on that new glass porch she put in."

"To glassed-in porches!" Buddy said, gulping down the last of his beer.

"And widows without kids," Eddy said.

"Eddy, what's the matter with you?"

"What do you mean?"

"We been friends a long time, Eddy. Come on. Tell old Buddy what's got you so low."

"It's Charles," Eddy said. "The boy hates my guts. I figured it would pass with time, but it ain't passing, and I don't know what to do. Shit Buddy, you got kids. How do you manage to get along?"

Buddy rustled around in the ice chest and popped the top on another beer. "Stuff in common, I guess. That's the key to it. You need some kind of thing you can share."

"The kid hates everything about me. Hates the business I'm in. Hates me being with his mom."

"Can't blame him for that last one."

"No, and I don't, I guess. But it's causing big problems between Cassie and me. If I can't manage to make peace with her boy, Cassie says we're through."

"What about baseball?"

"I tried that this afternoon. The kid shit all over me. Said I ought to plant a patch of pansies around home plate."

"So much for common ground," Buddy said. He eyed Eddy over the rim of his beer. "Old Buddy don't have all the answers, Eddy.

But he does know a little something that might lift your spirits some. A pair of newlyweds just bought that little brick bungalow over at the corner of Maple and Hope. You were talking earlier about the Dance of the Veils. From the way those two have been carrying on, it looks like they're trying to rewrite the *Kama Sutra.*"

"Go on."

"She gets home every evening at nine-fifteen. Starts shucking clothes the minute those high heels hit the drive."

"How's she look?"

"Loaded. And him waiting there in that sunroom like some kind of poster-boy for Oscar Mayer. Listen to Dr. Buddy, now. When you get done here, dump the kid off and drop by. It'll do you good."

Buddy climbed into his truck and roared off into the gathering gloom, empty beer cans pinging around in back like hailstones in a thunderstorm. Charles was done washing anyhow, and had taken to spraying cars passing by in the street.

They pulled out of Quirk's Dixie Quick Wash with the Braves on the radio. For the first time he could remember, Eddy was actually glad to be listening to a baseball game. That is, listening to Charles listen to one. Eddy's head was full of Cassie, and the third time he'd felt the warm, wet hand of Fate.

It had been a bright autumn day, way into the crisp end of the season, and the leaves off every elm in Kilbourne Heights lay like a golden welcome mat across Cassie's lawn. Eddy stood, rake in fist, his sole focus the naked teacher through the bathroom window grading papers in the tub. Red ink gushed onto the pages on the tray in her lap like the blood roaring in his veins. He couldn't move, couldn't look away—not even when he saw Cassie lock her eyes onto his. But she didn't close the blinds or call the cops, or even cover herself with a towel. Instead Cassie stood up, all slow-sliding suds and frothy curves, opened the window, then held out her hand

and helped him climb in. The entire fabric of Eddy's existence focused on the moment Cassie reached through that window and took Fate in her own hands. He'd spent his whole life on his knees, looking for a miracle. Maybe the time had come to make one for himself. He turned off onto Maple Street, headed in the direction of Hope.

"You did a good job back there, Chuck," he said slowly. "The car looks great."

"This isn't the way home," Charles said.

"That's true. There's something important we need to take care of together, before I drop you at your mom's."

"Got some pansies to plant?"

"Planting flowers, Chuck, is the second most necessary thing in life."

"What's the first?"

"Your mom."

Eddy's skin felt like a soaker hose and his heart was pumping sweat as he pulled into a dark spot at the corner of Maple and Hope. The dashboard clock read nine-thirteen. In the rearview mirror, the outline of Buddy Quirk's pickup filled the streetlight shadow of an elm. He cut the headlights and killed the engine, but left the radio on the game.

"Chuck, I've got to check for rootworms in these people's oleander hedge. I think it would make your mother happy if you'd come help me out."

"I'm transparent. You're talking through me."

"Fair enough. Just wait right here."

Eddy eased his way across the yard and settled in behind the hedge. He saw a car pull up, saw the sunroom door swing open, saw a pair of red high heels step out into a swath of yellow glare. He watched a red skirt crumple around the shoes. He watched a sheer

WHISPERS IN DUST AND BONE

red blouse go sailing, then a delicate red chemise. He took a careful look at Cassie's car—measuring the angle, making sure everything he'd been watching was visible to the boy.

It was. That is, it would have been. But for the life of him, he couldn't make out Charles. In a moment of real panic, he scanned the street for a white Braves jersey. He searched the yard, the driveway, the porch. He saw a man standing in the sunroom, two naked bodies folding into one. But there was still no sign of Charles. He wondered if his last chance at a life together with Cassie had just disappeared in the dark with her boy.

"Find any rootworms?"

Eddy jumped almost out of his skin. Then he caught a skipped-heartbeat glimpse of a baseball cap beside him, a gangling shadow sinking down on one knee and peeping through the oleander leaves.

"Chuck!"

"Shh!"

"I don't know what to say."

"How about asking me to help you plant some flowers?"

Four Smiles of Señora de Vega

The bus roars into Copacabana and the rumble of tires on stone streets can be heard only as an undertone of the music. Andean folk music howls on and on. It didn't even stop at the border—jangling on in the guardpost and whistling to greet us as we climbed back over Quechua Indians in black fedoras and chickens in cages and into our seat—and while we bounce over cobblestones and past garage-door shopfronts, flutes and whistles and stucco walls, tin and red-brown tile roofs, mandolins and guitars jumble all together until we pull into the *Plaza de Armas* and the clapping, chanting, singing dies with the bus.

"Bienvenidos a Copacabana!" the conductor says. *"Copacabana!"* The son of a bitch. Every cross-country bus in Peru and Bolivia has a

conductor as well as a driver to protect the passengers, keep an eye on the luggage, and take whatever he can get off the ragged poor who wait next to the road with their harvest bags full of coca leaves and their livestock, and dole out coins or food but receive no ticket—not even a seat, just a bare nod and a chance to force a spot in the aisle that is always already full. Today's conductor is short but wide, with a classic black-hat face from a Western movie. It is a face from which even the most heavily-armed Shining Path guerrilla might hesitate to steal.

He goes on rapid-fire about *comida y gasolina,* and about *una hora* and *cuarenta y cinco minutos,* and *el lago a visitar.* Then comes something about *cambio* and *el tiempo* and *el autobús que sale a las tres y media de la Plaza de Armas.* His dialect is hard to puzzle out. Our Peruvian conductor and driver were changed at the Bolivian border, and here in Bolivia the *Castellano*—the South American word for *Español*—sounds different from the Spanish they speak in Peru.

Everyone gets up, so David and I get up and push toward the front. I ask the conductor, *"Qué pasa con la hora y los cuarenta y cinco minutos?"* and he points at his watch, says something again about an hour, then about forty-five minutes and half past three, and I'm still not clear. But I don't much want to talk to the conductor—it being the conductor who howl-pitched the music, and when asked to turn it down gave me a blank stare and acted as though he'd never heard *Castellano* in his life—and Old Black Hat doesn't want to talk to me. He narrows his eyes and cuts them away out the door.

So we climb out into the main square of Copacabana, a town at the same time very high up, and very low down. Twelve and a half thousand feet up in the Andes Mountains it lies, and yet below the equator, so that spring comes in September and winter in June. It is December now. But the tops of the Andes, gray-white in the sun and black in shadow, show no sign of green. A couple of restaurants around the *plaza* have tables outside. We make sure our rucksacks stay in the cargo bin until the conductor locks the door, then ooze our way through the high air and pick a table to collapse into.

"Una carta?" a waiter says.

"You hungry?" David says.

"No," I say to the façade-faced waiter. *"Dos mates, por favor. Nada más."*

"Come to think of it," David says, "I might could eat a little something." His face is washed gray by the altitude, longish stubble dark against pale cheeks. But despite the busride and not sleeping, despite the *turista*—unbelievably fierce diarrhea really does attack every non–South American who drinks the water here—his neck and shoulders look as full now as the day we left home.

"You Coonass son of a bitch," I say. "I don't believe you've lost a single pound."

The waiter brings out two *mates* in white ceramic cups. *Mate de coca* is a kind of tea brewed from the coca leaf that is grown everywhere here as a cash crop for sale to restaurants, *narcotraficantes,* the overworked and underfed. You can go a whole day, they say, on the leaf alone. The *mates* are deep green and they taste like their color. There is nothing better for *soroche*—the lead-bellied, weak-kneed feeling two-plus miles of altitude gives to people who grew up on the bayou in Louisiana or in the Southwest Texas brush.

"You sure you don't want anything?" David says. "You look like you could use something."

"I'm sure. It looks like a downhill run all the way to the lake."

We flow away with the streets toward distant blue. The shopfronts give way quickly to housefronts where windowboxes thick with tiny red flowers, not quite open, are the only sign of the strange December spring. It's rocky by the lake. A couple of Indian women in blanket skirts and black hats squat on a stone and wash clothes. I sit on a rock warm with the sun and watch the women, watch the wind ripple the lake, watch David take off his shoes and wade out.

Green-and-brown reed boats bob in the distance and white-capped peaks seem to rise out of the lake above David's head. The water itself is that unbelievable blue only deep mountain lakes can be. Titicaca is the highest and deepest, and I've been waiting a life-time to sit and stare into this blue and listen to the steady scrape of wet cotton on stone.

"Come on!" David yells. "Come on and get in Titicaca!"

He splits the word in half, drawing out the two kid's curse words in the middle. *Titty. Caca.* There is a high hogback off to my right, ending in a cliff that juts out over the lake, and the words echo and re-echo off the rocks so that for a moment I seem to be surrounded by barefoot Cajuns calf-deep in curse words. The thought is enough to bring me to my feet.

"There you go!" David yells. "Come on in! The Titicaca's fine!"

The washerwomen ignore him. These high mountain people are the best at ignoring things I have ever seen. I make my way over the dry gray shore onto rocks that are black and wet. I kneel and touch water so clear I see the rippled shadows of my fingers on the bot-tom, water so cold it burns my hand.

"Catch!"

David's shirt comes flying, then his longjohn top, his pants—an amazing maneuver—and he stands there in yellow boxers with green-and-brown earths all over them, facing out into blue. I glance at the washerwomen, still completely uninterested, then back at David who is dogpaddling now, straight out toward the middle of the lake in his underwear. I remember the last time I went into the water, in Aguas Calientes at the foot of Machu Picchu. The water, so hot it brought sweat, so mineral-thick in the dark, reflected the light of a single bulb into the black Andean sky. And there were no wash-erwomen. No David. Only Vera and me, our bodies intertwined in the mineral spring, and the steam rising into the air.

But I don't want to think about Vera. So I take off my boots, roll up my jeans and wade out. The shock of the cold catches the breath in my chest. The rocks are covered with algae and there is moss on the soft bottom around them so that I have to hold my arms out away from my body to keep from falling. On the soft spots my feet stay planted and I can lower my arms to my sides. But like the lakeshore, the bottom is rocky. I lower my arms only to raise them again.

It comes to me that I no longer hear the scrape of wet cotton on stone and I look over my shoulder, expecting the washerwomen to be gone. They are still there, though. Both of them. And they are staring at me. Having paid no mind to the nimble gringo in yellow underwear tossing away his clothes, the awkward wading gringo captivates them. Their broad Indian faces never move.

"You look," David says, grinning and dogpaddling up close, "like some kind of crazy bird."

"*Tu madre,*" I say, as much to the washerwomen as to David, and lock my arms against my sides.

There comes a steady, high-pitched wail. A horn. It blows and blows, echoing off the hogback. David dogpaddles closer. His grin fades away.

"That can't be our bus," he says, "can it?"

"It can't be."

In short blasts now, one after the other, the horn sound echoes along the shore. Waist deep in water, David stands and checks his watch. "How long did they say?"

"The conductor said an hour and forty-five minutes."

"You sure?"

"He said half past three."

The horn starts to blow in alternating blasts. Short-long. Short-long. David strides past me through the water as easily as if he were walking on land. By the time my feet hit dry rock, he's lacing his boots. I sit as he stands, pants wet over his boxers, and races away without a word. Then the horn sound stops and twelve and a half thousand feet up in the Andes, uphill, I break into a sprint. My calves burn. My chest burns. My breath goes ragged. There are people now on the streets in front of the houses. They stare at me as I pass. Seeming neither to cheer for, nor pull against me, they watch as I race across the empty square to where a breathless gringo sits, head between his knees on the smoothworn stones.

"I came so close," David gasps, "I could smell the diesel."

I sink down beside him and breathe. Just breathe, seeing in my mind's eye two Yankee rucksacks on a Peruvian bus with a Bolivian crew on their way to an unknown location in La Paz.

"Everything's gone," I say at last. "We're screwed."

"No," David says. "The hell with that. Get up! Let's go!"

It comes to me, as David drags me to my feet, that one of the things in those rucksacks is our return tickets. Our discount tickets on a Peruvian airline that are non-refundable and closed-ended, so that the return date can't be changed. So that, even if we manage to get the tickets replaced and make it someplace where we can get more traveler's checks—and even if the amount of the checks is enough to cover new sleeping bags, clothes, toothbrushes, and the rucksacks themselves—we'll still be stuck here below the equator for almost a month with no money left for anything. Not even food.

After too many half-understood directions in dialect and too many wrong turns taken at a run, we find the combination long-distance telephone and bus office just downhill from the *plaza,* behind a white stucco façade. The old woman behind the counter stands and says, *"Buenos días,"* as we burst in.

David doesn't bother with good day. *"El autobús,"* he says, *"salió temprano."* The bus left early.

"No," the old woman says, and gives us the stare. She doesn't look like a Quechua Indian—she is dressed all in black, in a loose flowing skirt and a cardigan; her cheekbones are narrower, her skin lighter, her features more Castilian-looking—but the expression on her face is the same. She could just as easily be crushing roaches, or cooking eggs. *"El salió a tiempo. Exactamente a las tres y media."*

"On time?" I say. "But that's impossible! It's only three!"

"Son las tres," David says.

"No," she says. *"Son las cuatro."*

"Por favor," David says very slowly. *"No entiendo."* I feel as lost as he sounds.

"De dónde vienes?"

"De Perú," David says.

The counterwoman nods almost imperceptibly. *"El tiempo en Perú,"* she says, *"es diferente del tiempo aquí, en Bolivia."*

"Qué es la diferencia?" David says.

"Una hora," the old woman says.

"The time is one hour different here," David says. To me. And suddenly, like that lead-bellied *soroche* feeling, my talk with the conductor hits me again. "One hour, Mr. *Español.*"

"All right! It was my fault. Does that make you happy? Are you happy?"

"No, I'm broke. I'm dirty. My pants are wet. And everything I own is on the way to La Paz."

I don't dare look at David. I keep my eyes on the woman as I try to explain our problem, doing my best to find the right verbs, to translate nouns that, like the time, seem to have been altered by our border crossing.

"*No entiendo,*" she says after a while. "*No entiendo.*"

It's David's turn to try. I shift my attention away from the woman, up onto the blank stucco wall. It seems to care at least as much about our problem. Finally, David taps me on the shoulder. "There's no way to get to La Paz until tomorrow afternoon," he says. Then he turns back to the counterwoman. "*Hay un otro autobús mañana,*" he says. "*No?*"

"*Sí,*" the old woman says, "*sí hay.*"

Then David and I pool Spanish, ask if it's possible to call La Paz, talk to the hotel the bus will stop at, explain what's happened, and ask them to hold our luggage until we arrive.

"*Sí,*" she says simply. "*Es posible.*"

"*Dos preguntas mas,*" David says softly. Two more questions.

"*Sí?*"

"*Como se llama?*" he asks her. "*Y, por favor, hablarán por nosotros?*"

Her name is *Señora* de Vega, she says. It will please her to speak for us. Then comes a change in the counterwoman's face. Whether at David or his Spanish, she suddenly smiles. It is a close-lipped old woman's grin, difficult to decipher. It unnerves me almost as much as the thought of our return plane tickets in a luggage bin on the way to La Paz, guarded by Old Black Hat.

Señora de Vega puts our call in to the operator from the desk phone, and hangs up. After a while the phone rings again, meaning our call has gone through. I try to listen as she talks to the hotel, but she speaks with two or three different people, rapid-fire. I catch a few nouns, a phrase here and there. Finally there comes a pause that draws out, then a bit more rapid-fire Bolivian, and *Señora* de Vega hangs up the phone.

"*Por favor,*" David says. "*Qué dijeron?*"

Someone there will take care of our luggage, she says. Then she holds out a hand. *"Quinientos pesos, por favor."* The close-lipped smile has disappeared. *"Quinientos pesos,"* she says again.

It takes all I have to cover the call. So David and I pool more Spanish. Our traveler's checks are in our luggage, we say. We changed hardly any Intis into pesos at the border because the rate was so bad. We need to change what money we have left in our pockets to pay for a little food and a place to sleep. But the banks are closed.

Señora de Vega smiles a second time. It is that same dry grin, as impenetrable as stone. Go back, she says, and see the lake from the top of the cliff. Then she writes something on a piece of paper. Go on, she says, not to worry. Your things will be safe, you'll have a room for the night. Here, she says, and hands David the paper. When the bus leaves tomorrow, you will be on it.

"Gracias!" David says.

"But," I say, "the conductor—"

"Muchas gracias!" David says, taking hold of my arm and yanking me toward the door.

"The conductor took our tickets!"

"Yes!" David says, and shoves me out into the sun. "He did. But the *Señora* says we're covered." He seems to be taking her suggestion, dragging me downhill toward the lake.

"Then you believe her?" I say. "You trust her?"

"As much as I'll trust your Spanish, ever again."

I yank my arm away, muttering a phrase I learned as a boy. A Texmex curse, it has to do with David's facial anatomy and a donkey's body part. I find myself hoping it will make the border crossing better than the rest of my *Castellano*.

"Tu madre," David says.

Bingo.

"Look," David says, "I believe her. I mean, did you see that smile she gave us? Jesus, what a beautiful smile."

"She gave us two smiles," I say. "Two. I was counting. And I haven't had much luck, here lately, with beautiful things."

The top of the hogback is flat and stretches maybe a hundred yards. Widest back toward Copacabana, the bluff narrows toward the cliff like an arrowhead pointing away into blue. There are shrines here to saints. All concrete and stacked rocks and alcoves with white statues, the shrines have stone altars out front where plastic flowers in sunfaded vases stand among strewn blackened petals. At the base of the statues are framed photographs. Some in color, some in black-and-white, the photos are of people with no expressions on their faces.

It is the cliff that draws us. The bluff drops straight off into the lake a hundred feet below. From navy to indigo to a nameless color in the distance, the blue of the water seems to bleed into the sky—a color so strong it has a smell. The wind gusts sharp with the scent of blue distance and high mountain air.

A little below us on a narrow shelf of rock, a couple sits and snuggles, speaking German. *Der blaue, blaue See. Die Berge im Abstand.* The blue, blue lake. The distant mountains. I find myself thinking again of bodies intertwined in dark water. I feel Vera against me, the steam from the hot spring rising off our bodies. I see Vera's face looking out over Machu Picchu, then again staring out a window as I stand next to the train. In her eyes is that look she must have learned down here—empty as the high Andean plain and as indifferent, as though there had never been a night of dark water and skin sliding on skin.

It comes to me, looking out into the color the water and sky have become, that Vera and Lake Titicaca are exactly the same. Just two more in a long line of beautiful things I am unwelcome among. An alien. An unbeautiful stranger in a strange and beautiful land. The undecipherable smiles of *Señora* de Vega, the look in Vera's eyes as I stood beside her train, the blank Indian faces don't care whether I'm here or I'm gone.

"Let's go," I say to David.

"Wait a little," he says. "It's almost sunset."

"I'm going."

"You cold?" he says.

"Blue."

We make our way stop-and-go through the back streets of Copacabana, traveling streetlight by scattered streetlight and matching the penciled words of *Señora* de Vega to the names of streets painted on stucco walls. We find hers finally, a long way from the *plaza,* so dark and narrow we almost pass it by. Past shuttered windows of houses with windowboxes instead of lawns, David leads us two more blocks down to where a bare bulb shines over a door.

"Well?" he says. "What do you think?"

"Does it matter what I think?"

"That's the spirit!" David says. Then he steps up and pounds on the door. I listen to the echoes draw out up and down the street, half expecting a band of blank-faced *narcotraficantes* to appear at any moment, armed to the teeth. Finally the door opens a crack, the length of a chain. There comes the sound of a familiar voice, and *Señora* de Vega steps outside.

"Buenas noches," she says. *"Vamos al hostelería!"*

David and the *Señora* walk in front and I lag a little behind them, hoping she understands that we are almost out of cash. It's not just paying for the room I'm thinking of. Here in this pitch black alley far from the center of town, I find myself remembering the look in Old Black Hat's eyes like I was less than nothing—and it comes to me what an excellent racket it would be, tricking tourists into missing the bus and taking their luggage, then luring them away into the dark and taking everything they have left in the world, including their lives.

Señora de Vega stops at the back of a long, low stucco building. Bare bulbs burn above three of four doors. The *Señora* goes to the unlit door, fits a key into the lock, swings it open. *"Momentito,"* she says, and disappears inside. Then comes a flash, and the *Señora* reappears with her hands stretched into the air over her head.

I raise my own hands with a speed that comes from pure adrenaline and stand there looking for gunmen, watching the very worst of my worst nightmares come true. My hands stretch over my head as far as they'll go. My eyes dart in all directions. I see David's startled expression, the blur of his hands rising over his head. I see the corner of a bed and the bare white walls of a tiny room that, to my surprise, is empty—except for the black-skirted *Señora* still reaching for the sky.

It begins to sink in that her hands are holding something. A string. The cord on an overhead bulb. I drop my hands to my sides and look into the face of *Señora* de Vega, expecting her to laugh out loud. But it is as though she'd been expecting us to raise our hands like idiots the minute she reached up to flip on the light.

"Mira," is all she says.

There isn't space enough inside for all of us. A wooden chair takes up every bit of room that isn't already occupied by a double bed. The tiny bathroom—a toilet crammed into a closet with a sink to one side—looks as cold as the concrete floor.

"Le gusta?" she says.

"Sí," David says. *"Pero, tenemos sólo Intis de Perú."*

"No hay problema," she says. *"Cinco mil."*

I have to back out into the alley to get the wallet out of my pocket. Five thousand Intis. It's all I have left. *Señora* de Vega flips on the outside light so that all four doors are lit now with bare bulbs. *Todos ocupados.* A good night for the good *Señora*. Then she edges past me in the alley and heads back the way we came.

"All right!" David says.

"David," I say, "it's going to be a long, hungry night."

David nods toward the corner of the building. To my surprise, the *Señora* is waiting there. For the third time and apparently at us, *Señora* de Vega stands smiling that strange, close-lipped smile. *"Ven,"* is all she says.

"Come on," David says. "It's supper time."

The *Señora* leads us back through dark streets to the light over her door and then ushers us into the smell of food. *"Mi casa es su casa,"* she says. It is the first time in two months and more below the equator that we've heard those words.

"Red beans and rice," David says, as she leads us past the kitchen. "It smells just like home."

I remember David saying that when he was growing up on the bayou in Lake Charles, Monday was washday. The Negro women would put on pots of red beans and sausage to slowcook while they did their laundry, then make rice when they came home with clean clothes. For me the scent of red beans and rice smells like nothing in particular—there being no bayous in Southwest Texas, and no Negro women. And washday for my father and me was always whatever day he happened to run out of underwear.

"Televisión?" the *Señora* says. She leads us into a den with a floor-lamp in one corner flanked by two green vinyl chairs, a green vinyl love seat behind a hardwood coffee table, and across from the love seat, an old-fashioned TV. The tone of her voice makes the word a question, and at the same time makes us aware that she is proud to be able to ask it.

"*Por favor,*" David says.

"*La cena,*" the *Señora* says, will be a while. She motions toward the love seat and leaves us alone.

It takes a while for the set to warm up. It's one of those huge old consoles, the kind with the picture tube set into a wooden cabinet with speakers at both ends, a turntable hidden under a lid in the top, and plenty of space left over for all your favorite albums. The sound comes up first. It's strange to hear *Castellano* coming out of that old American TV. Then the picture fades in, and I realize things have taken a weird turn indeed. It's *Alf* on TV. Alf, the fuzzy space alien, shipwrecked in the American suburbs with a typical middle-class family.

"I told you everything would turn out all right," David says. "Didn't I tell you?"

I'm too surprised by *Alf* to say. The voice-overs are wrong. The voice of the cardigan-wearing, four-eyed father is much too deep and strong. It sounds more like the voice of my own father—a voice which during a bout of whiskey-drinking could change into a hoarse, deep-throated roar. The dubbing is off. The lips stop moving sometimes after the words start to come, and the words keep coming a long time after the mouths have stopped. And there is something wrong with the actors' faces, a thing so basic it takes a long time to place. Emotion. I see so much expression there. They're so different from the blank faces David and I are surrounded by that they seem more alien by far than the fuzzy, goofy face of Alf. So much so that, even though these are typical actors playing typical Americans in a typical middle-class home, I can't figure out who the real aliens are—the actors, the Indians, Alf, or me?

It's even a typical episode. Alf chases around after the neighborhood cats—his favorite food—and almost gets found out by nosy neighbors who are too dense to figure anything out really, even the true nature of the mystery meat on their frozen dinners. So, as usual, it all comes out okay in the end. As Alf himself almost ceaselessly says, "No problem." Except on the Bolivian version it comes out *"No hay problema"* instead.

The *Señora* comes in just as *Alf* is ending, carrying two plates piled high with steaming red beans and rice. She sets them on the coffee table in front of David and me, then returns with another plate which she puts on a TV tray in front of a corner chair. A third trip produces three glasses of water which go next to the plates. Even though the smell rising up off the food is heart-rending, it's the water I reach for.

"Es potable," I say, *"para nosotros?"* Is it safe for us to drink? I try to put into my voice the same tone of respect that *Señora* de Vega used to refer to the TV. *"Seguro?"*

"Sí. Hay una botella en la cocina."

"Qué grande?"

"Grandísima," she says. *"Toma."*

"Muchas gracias," I say, and drain my glass dry. As I stand, David drains his also, and hands the empty glass to me.

In the kitchen there is a gas stove, a refrigerator and sink, all white, and green formica countertops that match the green-and-white tile floor. A five-liter bottle of water rests upside-down on a stand in the corner. *Grandísima* indeed. For a long time there is only the feel of the water going down and the gurgle of the tank as I fill and refill my glass, hardly stopping to breathe. Finally I get a glass for David and follow the rapid-fire sound of TV *Castellano* back into the den.

The new program is *El Hombre Increíble*. The radiation-exposed American, Dr. David Banner, is on the run from the U.S. Army on Bolivian TV—and trying hard to stay calm. The red beans and rice is wonderfully spicy, enough to make my eyes water. There is meat in it also, but what kind I don't know. Around mouthfuls and during commercials, my own David, who is no doctor, tries to get the trick of the dialect. I divide my time between listening to David's attempts at conversation and the strange, not-quite-calm-enough voice-over of Dr. David Banner, who is no Cajun, on the Bolivian version of the show.

"*Qué carne es?*" Cajun David asks the *Señora*, nodding down at the food on his plate, which is almost gone.

"*Cabrito,*" the *Señora* says. "*Te gusta?*"

"*Me gusta mucho,*" David says to the *Señora*. Then he looks at me. "They'll never believe this back in Lake Charles. Red beans, rice, and goat."

I'm having a hard time believing it myself. Not the meat so much as the rest of it. The TV trays. The talking only during commercials. *The Incredible Hulk* on Bolivian TV. On the set, unCajun-like Dr. David Banner, in his not-quite-calm-enough voice-over, seems to be begging the Army guys not to piss him off. Finally, hard-pressed by the misguided gringos—who, poor un-lipsynched fools, seem to think they have him right where they want him—Dr. David Banner loses his cool. Lou Ferrigno, pumped up and green-painted, shreds his shirt and goes berserk all over the screen. The dubbing and the voice-over work much better for the Hulk than for Dr. Banner. The hoarse, deep-throated roar of the monster seems strangely familiar. Too familiar. The kind of roar that could come from anyone's den, between anyone's commercials, on either side of the equator—high up or low down.

Dinner ends with *El Hombre Increíble* and the *Señora* turns off the set. It's just as well. The Hulk, after beating the crap out of everyone and everything in sight, has disappeared. Dr. Banner is himself again, on the run alone. We sit in the den with our dinner dishes and try our best to communicate. David and I tell the *Señora* where we're from, where we've been so far, what things we've seen. The *Señora* tells us about her two sons. One is in the Bolivian Army, she says. The other manages a hotel in La Paz. The same hotel, she says, where our luggage will be waiting for us, *"seguro,"* when we arrive on tomorrow's bus.

But it's not long before our Spanish runs low, and as the *Señora* says, it's getting late. David and I offer to clean up the dinner mess. It's the least, we say, that we can do. But the *Señora* will have none of it. Go back to your room, she says, get some sleep. Then she smiles at us for the fourth time. Come to see me at the office tomorrow, she says, before you get on the bus.

"I told you so," David says, once we're outside among the windowboxes, his voice echoing off cobblestones and stucco walls and delicate red flowers. "Didn't I tell you? Everything's going to be all right!"

"No hay problema?"

"Right! No problem! Her son manages the hotel!"

"You sleepy?" I say.

"You crazy?"

"Maybe," I say, thinking for the first time how much that close-lipped old woman's smile is like a windowbox flower, not quite open but beautiful, a first tentative sign of spring. "But let's go down and have a look at old Titicaca anyway. What do you say? It looks like a downhill run all the way to the lake."

Earline's Combustion

At precisely 2 p.m. on August 27, 1983, Ms. Earline Redfern exploded in a scarlet sheet of flame. She flashed for an instant like the Fourth of July up out of the living room recliner she'd given Johnny and Gracie Bautista on their wedding day, and turned the picture tube blood-red before she ricocheted off the ceiling and seared the eyebrows off everybody in the room. Then the recliner caught fire and the mobile home was filled with dirty gray smoke. The stench was incredible.

Johnny sat on the couch with a beer in his fist and stared at the game through the haze. If he had been a churchgoer, he would've sworn the hand of God had reached down and brought his mother-in-law home to Glory to keep him from sending her there himself.

The Houston Oilers were losing their final pre-season game of the year to the Dallas Cowboys and everything Johnny had in this life, he had riding on the Oilers. He was six payments back on the double-wide and four payments back on his truck. Earline had bought up the notes, along with every other IOU with his name on it that was floating around the county, and they'd bet it all—his eight years of gambling and losing against her eight months with a Mexican son-in-law—on this one pre-season football game, winner take all.

"Win, and stay here with Gracie and the baby debt-free," was the way Earline had put it. "Lose, and nose that red pimp-mobile south and drive till your wetback ass runs out of country."

Johnny wasn't sure how long it had been since the Oilers went down by three touchdowns, and he'd started to pray. "Oh God, give me a miracle. Give me a miracle, and I'll change so You won't even know me. I'll give up the drinking, and I'll give up the gambling. Oh God, I'll give up football. Give me a miracle and I'll spend every dollar I earn from here on out, on my wife and my child."

"Miracle my ass!" Earline had shouted, and she'd laughed at that. "I got your Godda—"

Then Earline flashed fire and the picture tube went bloody and the whole world turned to smoke and stink. Johnny heard the baby start to squall and looked over just in time to see Gracie's mouth drop open and Hiram's Crown Royal drop onto the carpet. Gracie slung her beer one way, her cigarette another, and pressed the baby's tiny, precious face into her halter top. Hiram just sat and stared into the fiery spot. He'd been chasing Earline's bottomland for years.

Johnny guessed it must've been little Patsy's crying that set him in motion. He charged up off the couch the way he'd fired off the line all those high school football Friday nights, and hauled Gracie and the baby out onto the porch.

"Run next door!" he said.

Gracie stared past Johnny at the smoke that was pouring out the front door.

"Run next door and call the fire department!" Johnny said, his face so close to Gracie's now he could taste her hairspray.

But she just stood there and held little Patsy, and stared into the smoke like a back-up quarterback caught in the teeth of an all-out blitz. "Mamma," was all she said.

Johnny took hold of her shoulders and set off every word with a shake. "Run-next-door!" he yelled. "Call-the-fire-department!"

She twisted out of his grip, finally, and took off across the yard with the baby tucked away in both arms safe as a pearly-white pigskin.

"Water!" Johnny yelled. He took a deep breath and headed back into the trailer. "Get a bucket of water, Mr. Albright!" Through the smoke that felt like red ants in his eyes, Johnny saw Hiram sprint into the kitchen.

"Baking soda! Mamma always said there was nothing to smother a fire like a little Arm & Hammer!"

Johnny ran into the kitchen, snatched the mop bucket out of the bottom of the pantry, and started filling it from the faucet. He saw Hiram's face lit up in the refrigerator glow, hazy gray as the TV.

"Hurry up, Johnny! Hurry up, damn you!"

He saw Hiram's face wink out and heard him run into the living room before he felt the bucket finally start to overflow. Then he headed back into the living room himself, only to pull up short at the sight of Hiram Albright—town mayor and owner of most of the workable land in the area—standing next to the recliner looking scorched and hysterical, shaking a cloud of baking soda in the direction of the flames.

"Johnny!"

In her younger days, Earline had been a looker. She'd run

through a couple of wealthy older husbands like a three-hundred-pound fullback through a defensive secondary, and along the way picked up a herd of registered dairy cattle and the biggest chunk of bottomland in the county. You'd never have known it by the way she lived. The only one who'd ever seen a dime of that money was Gracie, and that was just to convince her to leave "that Goddamn greaser Johnny Bautista" and move back home with "her own kind." Johnny resented Earline. He resented the way that plush recliner took up a third of his living room, and the way Earline sat in it like it was some kind of throne, and ruled over what was supposed to be his castle. But he resented most of all the way Earline had stacked the deck against him. It wasn't enough, her buying up his notes and markers. She'd rewritten her will. If Gracie didn't part ways with Johnny by the time Earline's will was read, then Gracie would never lay eyes on another nickel, baby or no.

"Johnny!"

The game was still on. Johnny saw what looked like the Oilers finally scoring a touchdown as he tossed his bucketful of water onto the burning chair. The flames sputtered out. But the recliner went right on smoldering, the smoke so thick now he could barely make out the Oilers' point-after-try.

"Earline?" Hiram choked. "Earline, honey, can you hear me?"

The only response was the crackle of melting upholstery.

"I can't see a thing in there, Mr. Albright. I believe she's gone."

"Gone?" Hiram said. It was as though Johnny had a slow-motion replay camera pointed straight into Hiram's head. He saw the thought of Hiram losing his shot at Earline's acreage being blocked out by the fact that the chair she'd gone up in had been bought brand new at Albright Hardware. It was still under warranty. He watched the threat of the lawsuit roll over the promise of Hiram's upcoming state senatorial campaign like a Super Bowl contender over an expansion team. "Yep. I'm gonna run next door and see if I can't speed things up down at the firehouse. You stay here and do what you can for Earline."

Johnny re-filled the mop bucket easily enough, but he couldn't find the chair. The smoke was so thick he could hardly stand. The air tasted like burnt barbeque. He got down on his hands and knees, into the layer of breathable air underneath the smoke, and saw the bottom half of the TV screen slide into view just as a pair of tree-trunks in Oiler Blue launched themselves across a pile of silver-legged Cowboys and sailed into the end zone for another Houston TD. Then he tossed the water bucket in the direction of the recliner and crawled hard for open air.

Outside the sun flared white-hot in a molten metal sky. A group of trailer park residents—farm and ranch hands of Hiram's that he housed at a profit on this worthless outcrop of sand and rock—huddled on the sparse carpet grass like a crew of officials arguing a call. They crowded in on Johnny, and over the howl of the fire-whistle and the dogs howling back at it, asked question after question about what had happened to Earline.

"She just busted out in flames is all!" he said, at last. "Her, or that damned recliner. Like a can of gas when you put a match to it—"

"Hush up, Johnny."

"But—"

"Just hush up is all." Hiram seemed to have risen up out of the carpet grass. He took Johnny by one arm, leaned in close, and whispered in his ear. "We don't need no more talk about that chair, you hear?"

"You mean we ought to lie about it?"

"Not lie, exactly, Johnny boy." That cagey look Hiram always took on around election time slid onto his face like it was greased. "But we wouldn't want to say anything that might upset little Gracie, now would we?"

"No sir."

"Good boy. You just follow my lead."

About that time Gracie came running up to Johnny and threw an arm around his waist. "Is Mamma," she said, "is she—"

"Ease up, honey, you're mashing the baby," Johnny said. He felt Gracie loosen up her grip a little. Then he looked over at Hiram, who shot him a slow nod. "I don't know, honey. There was so much smoke and the game was on and I . . . I couldn't tell anything for sure."

Through the heat waves that danced around the ramshackle trailers and drought-blasted mesquites, Johnny watched a faded red pumper truck with the words CARLOTTA VOL FIRE DEPT in gold letters on both doors rattle up onto the grass and die. Three men in cowboy boots and khaki work shirts jumped off the back and ran a hose through the crowd. Then Hiram took charge, personally leading the assault on the smoking mobile home. In addition to his position as town mayor, Hiram served as volunteer fire chief.

Johnny stood with Gracie next to a bed of pink-and-white petunias she and Earline had planted together that spring, keeping back the curious and trying to ignore questions about Earline. The crowd members—friends, enemies, and long-standing acquaintances of the deceased—all had their own ideas about the strange and unearthly nature of Earline's demise. A few, despite Hiram Albright's repeated denials, were taking the stance that it was the recliner rather than Earline herself that had done the actual combusting. "Earline," they said, "just got caught in the crossfire."

But most of the crowd was having none of that. "Earline didn't get caught in no crossfire," they said. "Mayor Albright seen it all with his own eyes. It was her that set that chair on fire, and not the other way around."

Old Mrs. Carnes, proud mother to both a Methodist preacher and a registered nurse, had kept a pious eye on the carryings-on across the creek at Earline's for the past twenty years. She was convinced it was all an act of God. "That hussy took the name of the Lord in vain just one time too many," she said. "The real shame is that little girl of hers who started out to be so sweet, and then turned trash. Even as blind a fool as Johnny should be able to see that baby ain't no Bautista."

Johnny stood with one hand in the soft curve of Gracie's bare back and the other hand on the baby. He heard every word old lady Carnes was saying. But he'd heard worse from Earline. Besides, he loved Gracie and little Patsy—be they brown, white, or polka-dotted—and every hard word ever spoken couldn't change the feel of Gracie's skin.

The radio in the pumper truck was tuned into the game, and even in the middle of all that talk about life and death and God, there were people listening in. The Cowboys and Oilers played once a year for bragging rights to all of Texas. It was more like a playoff game than a preseason match-up and everybody in the state took sides, one way or the other. Johnny was sure the reason Earline had become such a Cowboy fan lay in the fact that he'd rooted for the Oilers since he was born. Hiram also took a Cowboy stand—he liked to stand just as close to Earline as possible. Johnny, though, could never be sure which side Gracie was on. She would always wait until the final seconds and pick the team that was ahead.

Johnny stood there next to Gracie and stared down into the flowerbed. But what he saw wasn't row upon row of pink-and-white petals slowly wilting in the welding arc sun. Johnny saw instead a wide expanse of Astroturf. He saw white-painted hashmarks. He saw men in gleaming helmets flying against each other like he'd dreamed of flying since his time in the Friday night lights had ended, and the gambling got started, and he'd shrunk down to just not-quite-big-enough, not-quite-fast-enough, dumb old Johnny Bautista, Mayor Albright's foreman, who once made All-State at tight end.

From what he could make out it was late in the game, and the Oilers were driving for the touchdown that would tie it. The sudden hush of the other listeners made him recall his bet with Earline, his prayer for a miracle, his promise to change. It seemed to Johnny, big and slow as he knew he was, that what had happened to Earline was the kind of thing men of science could explain. The kind of thing that could be quota-ized. Percentagized. Laid odds on. But if the Houston Oilers, with their second-rate passer, their slow receivers, their three-yards-in-a-cloud-of-dust playbook, could come back from three touchdowns behind the Dallas Cowboy Doomsday Defense—and not just tie, but win—that would be a thing no percentage could ever account for. A no-line match-up. The Hand of God. And he would give up trying to catch back hold of the sound of glory, the sweet whisper of pigskin thrown high and far into his outstretched arms.

Hiram walked out onto the porch just as the Oilers crossed the goal line for their third touchdown and kicked the extra point that tied the game. Then the clock ran down to zero. Johnny heard a cut-off cheer, mixed with a few groans, from the crowd around the pumper truck. Hiram shot a solemn wave into the sound of it as he started across the yard.

Gracie pulled away from Johnny and met Hiram in the middle of the flowerbed. "Then, Mamma . . ."

Hiram shook his head.

Gracie pressed her face into Hiram's chest there among the crushed petunias.

On the radio, they were headed into overtime. Men in khaki wheeled the stretcher across the yard and loaded it onto the pumper truck. The crowd formed a narrow aisle that the body—a little lump covered by a sheet, surrounded by volunteer firemen and Hiram Albright—rolled the length of as it passed. Somebody snapped a picture. Then Johnny saw Hiram and Gracie walk off a little way toward the empty creekbed that divided Hiram's wilderness of mesquite from the fertile bottomlands of Earline.

"Gracie, Gracie. Poor darling Gracie," Hiram said. He pointed across at Earline's red-tiled ranch house and the rich pastureland all around it. "It's such a shame Earline rewrote that will."

"What do you mean, Mr. Albright?"

"Call me Hiram."

On the radio, Johnny heard the Cowboys win the coin toss and elect to receive.

"What do you mean, Hiram?" Gracie said. She was still crying a little, and from where Johnny was standing, maybe five yards away from them, he could see the baby fret against her breast.

"Look around you, Gracie." Hiram waved an arm across the creek at the herd of registered dairy cattle that made black-and-white checkerboards on green fields as they grazed. He waved at the fat black-and-gold honeybees that droned around the stacked white boxes that held their hives. He draped the arm across Gracie's bare shoulders. "After suffering through my daddy's death, and your mamma's second marriage to someone other than myself, I renamed that creek the Little Jordan."

On the radio, Johnny clearly heard the Cowboys go on offense. To his right, Hiram stood with one arm around Gracie and the other around the baby. To his left, Earline lay at ease on the back of the pumper truck. Frozen like a linebacker by a play-action fake, Johnny felt his whole world—eloping with Gracie, taking the job as Hiram's foreman, the birth of little Patsy—go as hazy as the inside of the trailer after Earline's maybe miracle combustion.

"And?" Gracie said.

"Earline didn't have any family at all besides you, did she, Gracie?"

"None I know of," Gracie said, looking up at Hiram with an expression of anything but loss.

"Well then," Hiram whispered, almost in her ear. "If only . . ."

Johnny listened to the sentence trail off down the slope. He watched Hiram, Gracie, and the baby start out after it.

He heard the Cowboys driving, driving. He was thinking about football.

Leslie Pictured

Leslie saw hands. She saw pale, swollen hands climb fist over fist up the wrought iron railing out front. There was no way she could help but picture the feet that must go with those hands.

It was after 5:30. Past closing time. And she was out of there—off into the soft, pink-and-white dogwood-studded day she'd watched unfold through plate glass windows, in between strapping the contoured beds of Birkenstock sandals onto tourists' feet. Feeling the key in her fingers and watching those hands work their way up the front rail right at her, Leslie pictured turning and going. She pictured going without turning—just backing her way past the counter, up over the fitting floor, down between the cases of sandals and into the storeroom to hide the receipts underneath the green Dilpaco Wove envelope box the owner used as a cash drop, and duck out the back door.

But just then the old man dragged himself up onto the stoop looking bent and gray, and she was thinking, as grimly determined as white knuckles. She felt his eyes meet hers through the plate glass door. And feeling as trapped, suddenly, by those eyes as the old man himself was trapped by the railing, and by the dark-haired woman who hovered there on the stoop between him and the stairs, Leslie felt herself reach out and unlock the front door.

"May I help you?" she said.

"Yes . . . do you . . ." The voice sounded thick and hesitant, as though it might at that moment have smelled strongly of whiskey. But Leslie caught no whiskey smell. There was only the dogwood trees, the tang of the ocean, the feel of cool dry air flowing out of the sandal shop into the warm wet breeze blowing in off the sea. "Do you carry . . . the Birkenstock sandals?"

"Birkenstock sandals are the only kind of shoe we sell."

"How very . . . convenient."

"But we're closed."

"At what time did you . . . end your business day this afternoon?"

"Five-thirty."

"Hmm . . ." He glanced down at his wrist and she pulled her eyes away from his, over to the clock on the wall behind her. It was almost six.

"I'm sorry," she said.

"Yes, well. Do you . . . do business by mail?"

"By mail?" she said, talking through the crack in the door but avoiding the old man's eyes—eyes as deep and blue as the Southwest Texas sky. There was a picture of someone in those eyes that she didn't want to see.

"I would like to . . . pay for a pair of the sandals and have you . . . mail them out to me."

"What I meant to say was that, yes sir, we do the mail-outs. But that, no sir, it would be much better if you'd come back in to the store tomorrow." Monday. The single day the owner came in and took his turn at sandal-stuffing—and her only day off.

"No?" the voice said. Then it went on strongly, as though her own hesitation had given it a kind of leg up onto firmer ground. "I have a cancer, you see. I have a very difficult time getting out and around."

"I'm sorry."

"It's nothing to be sorry about. It's just that my feet give me . . . problems. It was my podiatrist's idea that I try a pair of your shoes."

"Your podiatrist?" she said. "How nice." But the whole time she was thinking, My God. My God. She got a picture in her head all of a sudden of pale, gnarled feet. She pictured them bloated. Cancered. Smelling somehow worse than other feet smelled. She pictured having to touch them—having to force them into the contoured beds of Birkenstock sandals, and strap them down. "Yes sir. Yes we do mail shoes. If you'll just give me your size."

"I'm a nine."

"A nine? That's your American size."

"Yes."

"Do you know your European size?"

"My . . . European size?"

"Yes sir," she said, thinking, Yes, yes, yes, almost like a prayer. "The Birkenstocks only come in European sizes."

"No. I'm afraid . . . it rather sounds as though I will have to come back down, doesn't it?"

"Yes sir. If you'll just come back Monday—"

"Excuse me," he said. "Excuse me, please." And there was some familiar thing in his voice that brought her eyes, once again, up into those sky blue eyes. "Please, can't you let us come in?"

It wasn't until he glanced down to gauge the step up into the shop that she looked at the rest of him. He moved slowly, one hand not quite on the arm of the dark-haired woman beside him and the other clutching the head of a silver cane. His back was bent but he held his head up very straight, as though he was unsure of his balance. Or as though his legs were hurting him. Or his feet.

"Hello!" she heard him say suddenly, at the same time out of breath and triumphant. "We have not been properly introduced! My name is Ben Covington. This is my daughter-in-law, Martha Covington. We would like to see a pair of Birkenstock sandals."

"I'm Leslie. Were you interested in any particular style?"

"What styles are available?"

Leslie stretched an arm out at the wall to her right, where all fifteen available styles of Birkenstock sandals sat displayed in taupes and browns on clear plastic shelves. "These are they," she said.

"She speaks grammatically! She must be an English major, over at the College."

"No sir. That is, I used to be. I graduated in December."

"Oh? You graduated in English?"

"Yes sir," she said, thinking, And I'm still selling sandals. In a shop called Arch de Triumph. On King Street in Charleston, South Carolina, just down from the Daughters of the Confederacy and the Slave Market. Twelve hundred miles from the deep blue sky of home.

"I myself was an English major, once upon a time." The old man leaned hard on the daughter-in-law as he stepped up onto the fitting floor. Leslie saw gray tweed slacks, and beneath them a pair of black loafers half covered by the bottoms of his pants. She made her eyes roam around the shop, away from the loafers. "My grandson has a pair with two straps in the front and one across the back, like these."

"Those are Milanos," Leslie said, not looking.

"But his straps are closer together. I don't think they're authentic, though. Perhaps some sort of pseudo-Birkenstock."

"Pseudo-Birkenstocks?" Caught off-guard, Leslie felt herself almost smile. "That's a pretty good word for it. I guess there are a lot of them around."

"He wants a pair of the real ones, but his father won't give him the eighty-six dollars."

"That sounds pretty father-like."

"Sounds more to me like one of my stingy sons." The daughter-in-law laughed, even though she must be married to one of them, and Leslie caught herself almost smiling again. "Perhaps I'll buy him a pair for his birthday, although they do seem a bit pricey."

That one she had heard before. Heard again and again, every Tuesday through Sunday of every week since she'd gone to work selling shoes. She pointed at the green-and-white cross-stitched QUALITY sign that hung next to the Birkenstock display. It read:

QUALITY ...

is like buying oats. If you want
nice, clean, fresh oats, you must
pay a fair price. However, if you can
be satisfied with oats that have
already been through the horse ...
that comes a little cheaper.

The old man laughed out loud at it, but Leslie was serious. The QUALITY sign was the main reason she'd taken the Arch de Triumph job in the first place. All those words about oats and horses blended together with the smell of leather sandals and put her in mind of the scent of tack and saddles, and horses, and hay. The green cross-stitched X's lined up on the white background of cloth reminded her of row upon row of crops in green fields. The sign touched off the picture she carried around in her head, in place of home.

"I guess you get what you pay for," she said.

"Yes, well . . . why don't we try on a pair of those . . . what did you call them?"

"Milanos. But why don't you let me size you up in a pair of the Arizonas, first? They're the easiest ones to size in." Less straps, she was thinking. Less contact. "Then I'll let you try on the Milanos. I promise."

"Leslie, I am in your hands."

"You said you wore a nine?"

"You remembered. Leslie, I'm touched."

Your feet will be, she was thinking. And remembering the cancer, the podiatrist, the picture she'd gotten in her head of those pale, bloated feet, she looked back just in time to see the daughter-in-law help him down onto one of the old wooden church pews that served as fitting chairs.

"You're not from around here," she heard the old man say, "are you, Leslie?"

"Excuse me?"

"I asked whether you might not be from around here. You see, I thought I detected a hint in your speech of parts unknown."

"I'm not from Charleston," she said.

"I thought not. Where is home?"

"You're probably about a 42, or a 43," Leslie said, just to keep herself from thinking. "We'll try a regular width first, and then maybe go to a narrow after that." She set a couple of boxes down on the soft beige carpet of the fitting floor, thinking, So far so good.

She opened the first green-and-white shoebox with the colors, materials and styles printed crisp and black in German—*dunkelbraun velour Arizona*—at one end of the box. She watched the old man lean down, pull off his soft black shoes, and expose his feet that looked . . .

They looked . . .

Dead.

And not all that freshly-dead, either. They were too white and swollen for that. The big toe on both sides had been forced inward and downward so that it was sideways to the bulge of the foot. The smaller toes twisted nearly upside-down so that the toenails, which she saw were painted a very tasteful medium brown, were almost underneath.

"It is called edema," he said. "The swelling is caused by fluid collecting under the skin. Martha here did the toenails for me. She said they looked like they were about to pop off."

Leslie heard the daughter-in-law laugh at this. But even though she could almost feel the old man smiling down at her with an expectant kind of smile—wanting her to laugh, and by laughing, make the sight of those awful feet all right—laughter was the farthest thing from her mind. She had caught the smell. It wasn't the no-socks-in-leather-shoes kind of sour-sweat smell she usually associated with strangers' feet. This was different. More antiseptic. The kind of scent hospitals use to try and cover the stench of suffering that wafts out of the rooms as you walk by.

Smelling that mix of antiseptics and pain, Leslie got a picture in her head, all of a sudden—the very picture she'd been trying not to see in the old man's eyes—of someone who'd grown up on a ranch like she had. He and his father halter-broke and saddle-broke and trained quarterhorses so you could rope and work cattle off them. A cowboy, he'd called himself, living a cowboy's life. Beautiful was what she called him, with big rough hands from gentling horses, and eyes as blue and deep as the Southwest Texas sky. Until one of the horses he'd been breaking fell on him and rolled, so that two of the vertebrae in his neck were crushed together. When she walked into the hospital room, he couldn't even turn his head. Only the eyes had moved, and the lips, and the muscles of his face. She saw the hands that had been rough and strong now pale and swollen, spread wide and lifeless against white sheets, and she fainted dead away. She came to in the nurse's station. White-capped faces looked down into her face. Smelling salts covered almost completely the stench of pain. She tried to see again in her head the way his hands had felt against her body, so rough and strong from gentling horses, and his eyes sky-blue and deep. But the only picture that would come was him para-lyzed in that bed. So she got up, pushed the faces away, walked out of the hospital—and never saw her cowboy again.

Leslie knelt on the soft beige carpet smelling the hospital smell and feeling the sandals heavy in her hand. She tried to tighten the field of her vision down onto the medium brown nail polish the daughter-in-law had painted. The daughter-in-law has done it, she told herself. You can do it, too.

That was what she was thinking when she reached out and took his feet in her hands—and was surprised to find that instead of soft and spongy, like she'd expected them to feel, the old man's feet felt almost firm. She struggled a little getting the feet lined up in the contoured footbeds before she got them to halfway fit. Then she started strapping them down.

"Does that hurt?" she said.

"I hardly feel them," he said.

"Can you stand up for me?"

"Anything for you, Leslie."

He struggled about half-way up before the daughter-in-law reached out to help him. But he waved her off, and made it the rest of the way up on his own. Then he and Leslie stood and the daughter-in-law sat, and they all looked quietly down.

Strangely, against the contoured lines of the ideal foot, the old man's gnarled hooves looked somehow better. No one's feet ever fit precisely into the ideal footprint, and trying to make them fit as well as she could was something Leslie was used to. She looked hard, studying them. But the sideways angles of the big toes and the way the smaller ones were twisted made it impossible to tell whether they fit or not.

"Shall we try a larger size, my dear?" The old man sounded plucky, like he thought his feet looked better inside the sandals, too. But when he tried to sit, he lost control of his legs. They buckled under him, and before she could reach out a hand, Leslie saw him plop down hard into the church-pew chair.

"Sir?"

"God damn, son of a bitch!" he yelled. It was a big, full-throated yell. A cowboy's yell, almost, and Leslie found herself staring again into deep blue eyes. "I'm young inside, you see." Then she saw him smile, and for the first time since she'd seen those pale white hands on the railing, she found herself smiling a little with him. He had managed, she was thinking, to catch her off-guard again.

After that Leslie helped him up and down. He had a very hard time. His breathing grew heavy again, even worse than before, and he hardly flirted at all. But through the whole fitting process, he held her hand. His grip felt surprisingly firm, but gentle, almost as though he was the one trying to help her. Like helping cows birth calves, she was thinking. When cows that were usually so wild you couldn't get close to them would lean back against your arms that were deep inside them, feeling for a head, a hoof, some sign of life— the longest arms on a ranch where there was no son, only a daughter, and the calves had to be born. That was the difference, she was thinking, between the suffering of people and animals. There was something in people that made them want to draw you into it, make you suffer with them. The animals just wanted you to make the hurting stop. Maybe that was why the old man's feet didn't bother her so much, now that she'd touched them. The old man didn't seem to want to make her suffer. The old man seemed to Leslie to have come to terms.

She managed to get the size down, finally. A 42 regular. They didn't fit perfectly, of course. But the old gnarled toes were inside the raised toe guards, and all the arch supports seemed to be in the right places. And remembering her promise to show him Milanos, she brought out a pair in cognac nubuck.

"They match the nail polish perfectly," the daughter-in-law said.

"You know?" Leslie said. "I believe they do."

"What did you call them again?" the old man said.

"Milanos," Leslie said. "In cognac nubuck."

"Milanos in cognac?" he said. "That's perfect! You know, Leslie, I once took a sailboat to Milan. A forty-foot sloop."

"Milan is landlocked, Dad," the daughter-in-law broke in. "It's inland."

"A comment worthy of your husband, my dear. At least Leslie here has the good manners to allow an old man to tell a tale."

"Please," Leslie said. "Go on."

"It was a forty-foot sloop. Blue and white, and beautiful. We started out in Athens and sailed around the Mediterranean Sea. To Istanbul. To Patmos, where John wrote the Book of Revelation. To Rhodes, where the Colossus used to be."

"That is something," Leslie said, "I've always wanted to do."

"It was glorious. Glorious. I was out there during World War II on a destroyer and I wanted to bring my wife back with me, afterward, and show it to her by sail. The sea is a totally different thing by sail. Sudden storms. Calms where it seems the only sound in the world is your own breath. We had to sail only during the day, because of the treacherous rocks. The Scylla, you know, and Charybdis."

"Sounds like difficult sailing," Leslie said. She had lived four years next to the ocean, and never sailed a day in her life.

"We did the sailing ourselves," he said. "The captain and first mate came with the boat, of course. But my wife and I were the crew. We stocked up a load of booze, and a good deal of the booze we stocked was cognac." He smiled down at the shoes. "But by the end of each day we were so tired most of it remained unopened."

Leslie looked at the old man standing there in his black sport-coat, gray tweed slacks, and the medium brown Milanos, and thought about the sea. She tried to get a picture of it. Of him. He wasn't the least bit like any other old man she ever knew. Not like any of her professors. Not like the owner of the sandal shop. Not like her father, who lived his whole life on a cattle ranch and died not long after the bankmen came and took it. No, not at all like her father, she was thinking, who never had it in him to come to terms.

"Was it lonely out there, Mr. Covington?"

"Lonely? No. We got in touch with other boats by radio, and the sailboat company told us that if we could get enough people together, they would put on a sunset concert for us, complete with lyres. On Rhodes, they said, very near where the Colossus once stood. We managed to get enough people together, and it was mar-velous. The traditional Greek music and the sunset turning the gray rocks and beaches and blue water the most amazing colors. Most of the cognac that got opened, was opened that night."

All of a sudden, through the thin white hair and edema and the bend in his back, Leslie pictured him young. Young and strong and just married, standing on a gray rock beach against the orange and red and gold Mediterranean sunset he'd first seen from the deck of a destroyer during the war. When she looked again at him standing there in the sandal shop, his shoulders looked almost broad.

"Have you done any other traveling?" she said.

"We lived in China for a year," he said. "But it was nothing at all to compare with the Mediterranean. It was inland. Landlocked." He half-smiled at the daughter-in-law. "And my sons were there."

"That may be, Dad," the daughter-in-law said, half-smiling back at him. "But you still haven't gotten to the part of the tale where the boat sails into Milan."

"You must excuse me, Leslie my dear," he said. "Martha is quite correct. We sailed around to Athens. Then finished up in Venice, and took the train to Milan." He reached out a hand to Leslie and she helped him down into the chair. "Which brings us back to the Milanos. I suppose that I must pay you for them. How did you put it earlier? Oh yes. You get what you pay for."

Leslie stood and looked at Mr. Ben Covington sitting there, but saw only her picture of the tall young man, the beach, the sunset sea. She didn't want the story to come to an end.

"I guess so," she said.

She helped him back on with his big, comfortable-looking black loafers. She took his credit card. When she carried the voucher over, she put it on the back-order clipboard to make it easier for him to sign.

"My grandson will be so jealous," he said.

"He'll raid your closet, is what he'll do."

"His feet are smaller than mine. Martha here is the only one whose feet are my size."

The daughter-in-law smiled at that. "I don't think they're me," she said.

"Anyway, make sure you keep your receipt," Leslie said. "The sandals come with a lifetime guarantee."

"If the shoes outlast the cancer, I'll give them to Martha. She can trade them in for another style."

Leslie felt herself hesitate again. Somewhere between the picture and the story, she had forgotten the cancer. "I'll have to make a note of that in my log," she managed, finally. "No shoe-switching."

"Impossible," the daughter-in-law said. "When this is all over, I'm moving to the Mediterranean. Whether your son comes with me or not."

"Bravo!" As the daughter-in-law helped him up, Mr. Covington winked at Leslie. "Thank you, Leslie my dear. My address is right there on that voucher. Don't be a stranger." Then he met her eyes full on. "And now I think it's time we all went home."

She didn't walk him to the door. While the daughter-in-law helped him out onto the stoop, Leslie stared through plate glass windows into the afternoon that was dying in orange and red and gold. But she didn't see it. She couldn't even speak. Couldn't say goodbye. Mr. Ben Covington edged, white-knuckled, down the wrought iron railing and into the night that was falling on King Street. Headed home, he'd said. She couldn't see that either, couldn't find the picture she'd carried in her head all these years like a childhood prayer, of the only home she'd ever known. It seemed to Leslie that the sky itself had turned into a picture—a young man with blue eyes that had gone shallow and hands swollen white that had been rough-brown from gentling horses. That picture grew until it filled the plate glass windows, and grew, until it filled the whole world outside completely, and Leslie snatched the keys up off the counter and locked the door tight against it. Only then could she turn away, and look back into the Arch de Triumph at the QUALITY sign cross-stitched in row upon row like green fields she couldn't see.

Someone to Watch Over Me

He was waiting, but it wasn't raining.

There were stars out, even though with all the light coming up off the city you could hardly see them, and he was feeling okay through the first hour, but then it turned into an hour and a half. He had driven six hours north to get to Dallas and a half hour west to Valley Ranch, and it was beginning to seem like eight hours of unmet expectation.

She was playing softball.

At least that's where she said she'd be. And while she was out God knew where, doing God knew what all, here he was stuck in a parking lot square in the middle of God knew how many other parking lots—sober—but stone-drunk in love, listening to beer-drinking music and hoping for a crumpled fender or a couple of flat tires.

He was sitting underneath the area light outside her apartment when the two-hour mark went past. It was midnight, and he swore to himself that, love or no love, he would start the drive back home at 12:15 A.M. She said she'd leave a key there in the window. And when she said that she'd be home by ten o'clock, he'd assumed that ten o'clock meant 10 P.M. But at 12:15 that window was every bit as dark as the empty place he could feel swallowing his insides and he was wishing more than ever, if not for an honest-to-God collision, then for a whiskey-drunk. There was nothing like a whiskey-drunk to kill the pain.

He'd sworn that he would start the trip back home at 12:15, but extended his deadline to 12:30. And sitting there on the truck hood at 12:45 A.M.—engine running—listening to his third "just one more" Willie Nelson song in a row, he'd long since given up on bourbon and bad luck, and gone to wishing for a little necessary resolve.

When she pulled into the parking lot at 12:55, it was only two songs later. She slipped out of the car like a little girl who had dressed up in Daddy's softball suit and snuck out for a spin in Mamma's midnight blue Eldorado. He was fairly certain, truth be told—although he'd never seen the pink slip—that the name the car was in was really hers and not her mother's. But he was willing to bet the name inside that softball suit wasn't her father's. And he was positively sure it wasn't hers. After wondering for a while whose name it could have been though, and why, he decided that it didn't matter. The only thing really important was that it wasn't his.

He settled for the promise to be cold as a February 5 A.M.; strong enough to ignore all due apologies; man enough, when they came, to dry her tears. But she walked away from the Eldorado with her head held high, and instead of rushing right up so he could cut and wilt her, that wayward flower headed straight for her apartment without a nod in his direction.

Forgotten. She'd forgotten.

He managed to catch up to her at the foot of the stairs without ever quite breaking down enough to bust into a run. He saw the beer in her hand. He smelled the beers on her breath. He tried to keep his eyes trained on the softball uniform that was gray and red, and that looked to have been made for two or three of her.

He wanted to know what had happened, just exactly, to the year's worth of "missing," and "needing," that she'd cried about on the phone. "Trusting," he didn't even want to think about—there hadn't been scratch one on her car. But the only thing there was, once he was close enough to feel the stitching, was the way Mary seemed to fold into the flannel.

The next thing he knew they were drinking screwdrivers.

The O.J. was in the fridge. There was vodka in the freezer. Could he mix the drinks while she handwashed just a couple of dirty dishes? Dishwashers took "such a toll on the environment."

"Glasses?" he said.

She was "crushed" that he'd forgotten. Her nice glasses, she said, were over the sink where they had always been.

"The apartment looks smaller than the one in San Antonio."

The apartment was so "teeny" Mary said, she could hardly stand it. Did he need a just little more vodka in his screwdriver? She could hardly taste the vodka for the O.J.

"Okay."

The drive in to work took forty-five minutes if she got up early and missed the rush hour, and she had to set her alarm, every morning, for six o'clock. But she loved her job. She had her "own little cubicle" with windows for walls—all the cubicles were like that, for teamwork, everybody seeing everybody else and knowing they weren't alone—and her own desk, the one in the middle of all those other desks, with her own phone. He could go ahead and make himself at home, she was almost done with the dishes.

"The furniture in the living room looks familiar."

"Threadbare," she said, was more the word for it. She was counting on Daddy for a brand new suite, but in the meantime she would
have to "make do."

He sat on the floor, eased his back against the couch, and listened
to her clink dishes together. He'd doctored calves all morning long,
right on through lunch into the white-hot afternoon, and watched
the sun go down out the driver's window of his pickup. He could
still feel the weight of every wormy calf he'd thrown and held and
vaccinated without pause, and the bruises from every kick that had
connected. But there were worse things than working with cattle.
One of the buddies he'd grown up with had broken his neck instead
of the cowhorse he was trying to train, and another had gotten elec-
trocuted turning on an irrigation motor. He guessed all the ones
with any sense had gone off to the city, gotten their own little cubicles, and stayed. Through the window in the partition, he saw fluorescent light shine in Mary's hair.

"That San Antonio apartment sure looked to've been neater," he
said.

Mary had "no concept."

"The clothes," he said, "laying all over everything."

"Are Rebecca's," she said. Her hair moved out of the window.
He heard the icebox door.

"Rebecca?"

The girl she was thinking about moving in with, which was why
she was counting on Daddy for the new suite of furniture. Although
Daddy, she said, was against the move. Daddy was always against
everything. What did he think?

He didn't want to talk about her daddy. He wanted to talk about
the two of them. About San Antonio. About why on earth she'd

called him up and cried and said what she'd said. About why she'd asked him all the way up here if all she wanted to do was dishes. About how much she'd changed.

"I'd have to hear more about Rebecca before I could say," he said.

It was the most awful thing. Rebecca, she said, had driven down from California to live with "Cokie."

"Cokie?"

Cokie. She came down to live with him and he seemed like a really "neat guy" but, well, it turned out that Rebecca had driven all the way to Dallas just to find out that she "needed room." Which was why she'd told Cokie that she would be spending the night with Mary, but was really going out with Michael, who she'd met her first day at work.

"Poor Rebecca," he said.

"Excuse me?"

"Nothing. How did you meet?"

She laughed, that was the funny part. She was the one who had introduced Rebecca and Michael. Rebecca had walked into her office looking for "temporary secretarial" not five minutes after Michael had phoned for a secretary/receptionist for his real estate firm, who was "attractive," but "level-headed" and "a real go-getter." Anyway, she and Rebecca "did lunch," had "one or two too many," and "went on for hours," and here it was only two weeks later, and she and Rebecca were talking about moving in. That was the best thing about her job. There was always someone close for her to talk to.

He was about to stand up and walk into the kitchen just to get a little closer to her himself—although God knew how much he could use another drink—when he heard water start to drain, then heard the icebox door again, and in she came carrying two more screwdrivers. They looked more clear than orange.

It was so hot, she said as she handed him a glass, she could hardly stand it. She needed a change, that was what she needed. She needed to go for a swim.

"I don't have any shorts."

"No problem," she said, and went into the back. She came out wrapped in a blue-green towel that he remembered and tossed him a pair of polka-dot swimming trunks that she said were her brother's. But when he was finished in the bathroom—filled with other blue-green towels that he remembered and a box of dried rose petals he would never forget—the shorts hung loose around his waist. And he was twice the size of Mary's brother.

The only stop they made was at the icebox and when he dove into the pool, all the way to the bottom, the water felt as cold as the screwdrivers Mary had made. It was quiet, the water smooth and quiet, and all along the bottom there were lights that were warm. When he surfaced, the outside air that had been hot and dry felt cool. Mary sat on the edge of the pool as he swam over, on a towel that she had folded, and dangled her feet in the water.

"There looks to be a good bit less there of you," he said, "than I remembered."

The pace, she said, had been a little "fast" lately. She finished her drink and started in on his. She could hardly stand it. Things in San Antonio, she said, had been so much nicer, before they started "speeding up." Did he remember that time, when? And that other time, when? And the zoo? The Fiesta? All the parades?

"Yes," he said. But he didn't remember.

She kept on remembering things. Things that never happened—or else, never happened with him—and the empty place that had opened up in the parking lot kept swallowing more and more of him inside it, all the way back upstairs into her room. It was the same bed. And she was tired, she said, up since six o'clock and worked all day. But not that tired. . . .

"No," he said.

She didn't say anything. Started . . .

"No," he said again. "Tomorrow night."

Somewhere things kind of faded out. When they faded in again, it was almost daylight.

He lay there and felt her head on the empty place in his chest, and thought about the last time he'd felt the softness of her hair against his neck. It was on the couch at his father's house, on a Saturday morning six hours south and a year ago, eighty miles and more from the San Antonio city lights. She was supposed to have been there the night before. And he'd been lying there fearing flat tires, crumpled fenders, worse. Until the rain started coming down hard from the northeast, where she was supposed to be driving in from, and he figured, what with the bad roads and all, she'd turned back. So he lay there kind of dozing, thinking about the sound of rain and the way it smelled like security, and not having to work until the ground was good and dry. He figured he would call her in a couple of hours or so. But just as it was getting light, in she came and put her head on his chest, and said she'd just "been with" some other guy. He felt her hair damp against his neck, and felt his chest empty underneath it, and said, "You're nothing but pain." Then she was gone and his chest was wet and he smelled the rain.

It seemed to him, lying there six hours north and a million miles distant in the bed he remembered, that he was as empty as the sky before stars. All her time she didn't spend saving things, Mary put toward causing pain. There was no way around it.

When he walked down her stairs, it wasn't raining. He opened the truck door and the sky was empty, the sun just starting to pale the horizon, the city lights.

The Hat

The man on the ladder felt cold fingers of breeze take hold of his hat. He felt the hat fly up, felt the ladder shy away. And feeling the world sway, and him with it, he clamped both hands onto the top rung and held on. The wind whined in the wires. The dead traffic light swung sideways there where his hatbrim had been. He smelled the air from high up and watched the hat sail away into it, watched the hat disappear among thunderheads. Then the gust died, and the light swung away, and the world swayed back, and he eased down onto the bed of the truck.

"Looks like it's gonna take us both," he said.

"Like hell, Clint Mixson!" the man on the flatbed said. He had one hand on the ladder and one hand firmly fixed on the hat that was still on his head.

"I don't suppose, while you were standing there holding that bird's nest instead of the ladder, you troubled to notice where that bastard norther took my Stetson?" Clint Mixson said.

"South."

"You don't say."

"Yesir. Due south and high up. Kind of like a white felt goose. You might see it up there, when you climb back up to change out that traffic light."

Clint Mixson Moore looked south, at the mostly tin roofs of downtown Carlotta. He looked at the old railroad depot, graffiti-slathered and falling apart; at the boarded-up business fronts and broken windows; at the empty parking lot of Moore & Son Grocery. He looked back north at the line of thunderheads bearing down, bright white in the morning sun.

"Weldon," he said. "Do you want this prison or don't you?"

"Yesir," Weldon said.

"To get this prison, we have to win that vote tomorrow. And to win that vote, we have to get those dead flashing lights down and the new cycling lights up. Now. Before the church crowd comes through."

"That we do."

"All right, then. When we both climb up there," Clint Mixson said, "you can help me look for my hat."

"You're acting mayor," Weldon said. He took off his hat, brushed a sleeve across his forehead, put the hat back on. "But if you're on the ladder, and I'm on the ladder, it looks to me like we're gonna need somebody to hold that ladder. And with the Constable sitting down there at one end of town, and Johnny Bautista at the other, wouldn't you say that puts us in kind of a tight spot for ladder-holders? That is, unless you plan to leave one end of town open for them eighteen-wheelers to highball through."

Just then, as though every trucker between them and El Paso could hear every word Weldon said, the first big rig of the morning heaved into view. It rounded the curve at the west end of town—highballing, overloaded, and trying to avoid the weights and measures division of the Texas Department of Public Safety—and roared right at them. And even though the Constable was stationed up that way in his squad car, and the rig couldn't have been doing more than forty or so as it lumbered through the intersection, the wake of its passing made the flatbed shudder.

"Well sir?" Weldon shook a smoke out of the pack in his shirt pocket and lit up. "What does Your Acting Honor say to that?"

Clint Mixson squinted through the cloud of lungsmoke that billowed out into the diesel breeze. Sidling around the corner of Albright Hardware in their direction, he had just caught sight of a bent old man. In front of him, carried at arm's length in both hands, was the cloud-colored, thunderhead-shaped object that Clint Mixson had last seen sailing away into the sky.

"I'd say we just found my hat," he said.

Shorty crossed the lumberyard parking lot clutching the bright white something that had sailed down out of the sky and come to rest at his feet. He held the something out as far as his arms would reach, not so much to see what it looked like—it looked like a white felt Stetson, any fool could see that—as to make sure it felt true. Shorty had seen things fly down out of the sky before, or ride along in it, that had been solid enough to look at. But when he reached out a hand to touch them, it went right through. So he was walking along kneading the stiff-soft brim and taking the measure of the true that was in it from the way the felt snagged the callus-horned hide on his fingers, when he caught sight of what looked to be a flatbed truck with a stepladder and two men on the back of it, square in the middle of Big Road.

"Shorty!" he heard. "Hey Shorty, come here!"

Shorty eyed the maybe-truck. He looked hard at the maybe-ladder and the two maybe-men there on the back of it. One of them looked to be having a smoke. That one had on a tan straw cowboy hat. The other was hatless. The hatless one doing the yelling waved now for him to come over. But Shorty didn't want to come over. He didn't like the look of the one without the hat. He went still as a cat, hunting around for a bush or a hole or some kind of a thing to put the hat into. There was only gravel and grass, and the maybe-man waving now like he aimed to sail off into the sky himself. Shorty waited a little, kind of halfway hoping. But the maybe-man never lifted off even an inch. Finally Shorty snuck the hat around behind him and walked out into Big Road.

"Better watch out on Big Road!" Shorty yelled up at the maybe-men. "Better look both ways afore you cross it!" The first thing he did, once he got close enough, was hook a finger under the bumper and weigh the maybe-truck for true.

"What the hell is he yammering about?" the hatless one said.

"I never could understand him," the other one said and blew smoke.

Shorty eyed the men again. He didn't need to weigh them out. He'd latched onto their names. Clint Mixson Moore doing all the asking and Weldon Jackson in the tan straw hat with the smoke. Weldon Jackson had built the drug store a pretty good ways back and still had it running. Clint Mixson Moore had the grocery store. Shorty recalled one particular time when Clint Mixson Moore and a couple of other big boys got him drunk on malt liquor and painted his hair purple. Clint Mixson Moore hadn't built the grocery. He'd got hold of it when his father passed.

"Shorty! Hey, Shorty-boy!" Clint Mixson Moore said. "What've you got stuck away behind your back?"

"A something."

"What kind of a something?" Clint Mixson Moore went buzzard-eyed. "My hat?"

"Shorty's. Came down out of the sky to Shorty and that means it's Shorty's."

"Is he drunk already?" Clint Mixson Moore said.

"Not any drunker than the Constable," Weldon Jackson said. "And it sounds to me like the man might have a point."

"I thought you said you never could understand him."

"I never could."

"Shorty," Clint Mixson Moore said, "give me my hat."

"Shorty's."

"No, Shorty. That hat belongs to the mayor. Hiram Albright gave me that hat. You remember Mr. Hiram? He used to be mayor. Now he's gone off to the State Senate in Austin."

"Albright's all right."

"Hey!" Clint Mixson Moore said. "That sounds like Hiram's old campaign slogan. That's not bad! Hey Shorty-boy, can you say 'Prison for Progress?'"

Shorty pursed his lips and made the kind of sound a horse makes with his tail end when he's been on oats too long.

"Retard son of a bitch."

"Easy there, Clint Mixson," Weldon Jackson said.

"Okay, okay. Shorty, I'll give you five dollars for it."

Shorty made the horse-fart sound again.

"Ten dollars."

This time Shorty made a sound like the tail end of a cow.

"Give me back Hiram's lucky Stetson, and I'll give you twenty dollars. And I promise to buy you another one just like it."

"One out of the sky?" Shorty said.

"Cross my heart," Clint Mixson Moore knelt and said softly. "One out of the sky."

Clint Mixson reached the twenty dollars down and felt Shorty snatch it in his raspy old man's hands. But his eyes were on the hat. It seemed to rise on its own instead of being lifted. It seemed to leap into his grasp. Clint Mixson turned the hat over and over, working and reworking the smooth felt brim. Then he shot to his feet, flashing the hat over his head.

"What the hell do you think you're doing?" Weldon said.

"You want him holding that ladder?" Clint Mixson said.

He saw Weldon glance at Shorty standing there in the middle of the intersection, wild-eyed and toothless, staring up at the white felt arc against the lowering sky.

"I didn't figure so," Clint Mixson said.

He swung the hat back and forth, looking down the highway at the last building in town—an old caboose Hiram Albright had bought off the railroad when they pulled up stakes, and turned into a Texaco. Besides the broken-down depot slow-rotting in the grocery store parking lot, the Red Caboose Texaco was the last remaining vestige of Carlotta's railroad dream. When that slow train made its final trip through town, they'd picked up the tracks behind it.

"Clint Mixson?" Weldon said. "I want you to think about something."

"I am thinking about something," Clint Mixson said.

"Listen to me, now. If you're on the ladder and I'm on the ladder, and Johnny Bautista is holding that ladder, who do you think is gonna wait down at the Red Caboose and slow them rigs?"

"Shorty."

"You can't send Shorty down there alone to slow big rigs on that highway, Clint Mixson."

"Why the hell not?"

"Shit, Clint Mixson, it's Shorty!"

"I believe you've lost sight of what's at stake here," Clint Mixson said. He pointed at the PRISON FOR PROGRESS banner draped along one side of the flatbed, flapping lightly in the freshening breeze. "If we don't win that vote tomorrow, we lose every penny of that prison revenue Hiram worked so hard to get us. Look around you, Weldon. Without that prison, this town is dead."

"My parking lot's as empty as yours, Clint Mixson."

"There you go." Seeing Johnny Bautista pull out of the Red Caboose, Clint Mixson eased the hat back onto his head. "Besides, Shorty knows all about that highway. Don't you, Shorty?"

"Better watch out on Big Road! Better look both ways afore you cross it! Shorty can slow them rigs. If he has a smoke."

"You hear that, Weldon? How about a smoke for our new traffic man? What do you say?"

Weldon shook a cigarette out of his pack and handed it to Shorty. He reached out and lit it with the butt of his own smoke. "I think Shorty would've said anything to get that cigarette."

"Dammit, Weldon! Shorty knows how to take care of himself. How about that soap-in-a-sock?"

"How about what?"

"That bar of soap he always carries around stuffed in the end of a sock. The one he used to help the Constable out of that tight spot back when the Red Caboose was robbed. You know. The Constable down, and Shorty hit in the head with a pry bar, but managing to run the robbers off with that soap-in-a-sock. How about that?"

"Shit, Clint Mixson, that's just a story!"

"Well then," Clint Mixson said, recalling a peculiar hollow spot in a head of gnarled hair filling slowly with purple dye, "how'd he get that dent in his skull?"

"He got kicked almost dead by a horse."

Johnny Bautista pulled up then, his bright red Ford pickup spraying gravel as it slid into the intersection. "Anything the matter?" Johnny rolled down the window and said.

"A change of plan is all," Clint Mixson said. The stale beer and smoke smell coming off Johnny made his belly do a flip-flop. It seemed like Johnny had been on an alcohol and tobacco diet ever since the day Hiram Albright married his ex-wife.

"What kind of a change?"

"For starters, you can give Shorty your traffic flag."

"I can't do that, Clint Mixson."

"Why the hell not?"

"Remember how you said for me to bring a white handkerchief this morning that I could wave and slow traffic?"

"Go on."

"I got no handkerchief," Johnny said.

Clint Mixson looked from Johnny to Shorty to Weldon. He looked from the burned-out lights hanging over the highway to the line of thunderheads. "I'm taking suggestions," he said.

"Why not," Weldon said, "let our new traffic man here wave the acting mayor's white felt Stetson as a traffic flag instead of a handkerchief?"

"I can't do that, Weldon."

"You know?" Weldon said. "I believe you've lost sight of what's at stake here."

"All right, all right." Clint Mixson pulled the hat off. He looked at it. Turned it over. Looked at it some more. Then he handed the hat down.

Shorty latched on with both hands and headed for the caboose end of town. Walking along and feeling the brim stiff-soft against his gnarled fingers, he felt like he could sail through the air himself.

John Wayne wore a white Stetson. And Roy Rogers wore one. Shorty remembered that from the TV in the drugstore, where he could always sit on a hot Saturday afternoon with the chocolate malted Weldon Jackson let him have and watch the Westerns come on one after the other. Hopalong Cassidy wore a white felt Stetson back before there was such a thing as TV. The way they told it made Shorty see the hat, even though Hoppy came over the radio. Shorty recalled even farther back, when there'd been cowboys in this country. Real cowboys who lived out in the mesquite and prickly pear, caught wild horses, and rounded up longhorns that they drove to the railhead to sell. He wished they could see him now.

Shorty stood next to Big Road and waved the hat east the way Clint Mixson Moore said. He felt the wind gust out of the north fresh with the smell of whitebrush in bloom and the hat felt like a part of his hand. Shorty remembered wearing a white hat himself. It was foggy as the somethings he sometimes saw sail through the air when there was no malt liquor, but the sweet smell of whitebrush flowers took the measure of the true that was in it. Shorty recalled riding out in the thickets and hazing mustangs into hidden corrals. He recalled the whitebrush that bloomed so purple and sweet for so short a time. He recollected Mexican vaqueros who named their corrals after saints, and all the dark-eyed, dark-skinned girls he'd seen bloom so often, so early, and so quickly fade. Shorty swung the hat and smelled the wind blow sweet. He remembered wild horses.

Clint Mixson felt the north wind gust hard against him and felt again cold fingers of breeze. But with Weldon there below him, and big Johnny Bautista holding the ladder in both hands, he felt the world hardly sway at all. He had the dead light all but unbolted— three of four nuts off, and the last one loosened—and when the wind gusted again it swung the light in his direction just as he eased the last nut off, so that the whole thing slid free into his hands. Clint

Mixson held on, feeling the weight of the traffic light slowly drag him toward the asphalt fifteen feet below.

"Weldon," he said, "take hold!"

"No, hell no. Hell no."

But Clint Mixson saw Weldon unhook an arm from the ladder and hug the light against his chest like a neon-yellow teddy bear. He saw Johnny reach up and get a hand on the bottom.

"Now let go, Weldon. Let go!"

Weldon let go, and Johnny guided the light down onto the bed of the truck. Clint Mixson felt like howling out at the sight of it, but didn't want to lose the momentum.

"Now hand me up one of the live ones!"

Sure enough, Clint Mixson saw Johnny lift one of the new cycling lights up to Weldon, who squeezed it tight against his chest. He took the light away from Weldon and pulled it up onto his knee, then onto his shoulder, then on out into space. He mated the brack-etplate at the top with the plate dangling from the wire, squeezed all four bolts into their places, and snugged the nuts up tight. Then he let the light swing free—and witnessed the rebirth of Carlotta as it cycled from red to green.

"All right!" Clint Mixson howled. "All right!"

Shorty stood out front of the Red Caboose waving the hat and hearing Clint Mixson Moore howl. He didn't know what was happening exactly, but he liked the sound. Just then he saw a big rig come charging over the hill like a cow out of a patch of brush where her calf was hid. But instead of looking around for a tree or a fence to climb, Shorty waved the hat and stood his ground. Sure enough, less like a mother cow than a horse charging, the thing slowed up and went around. There came another one behind it. Shorty stood his ground and waved the hat, and saw that one slow, too. And veer. When a third one came, Shorty faced it down and saw it veer and follow the others into town.

Shorty felt a good foot taller and six inches thicker through the chest. Across Big Road he saw some red Herefords poke their pasty faces through the fence and go to cropping roadside grass the way cows will. He charged, waving the hat and letting fly a whoop out of his mustang days. The cows yanked their heads back through the barbed wire, turned tail, and ran away. Shorty looked around feeling tall, tall. He caught sight of some doves spooking up ahead of the frontline, coming in ones and twos and whining their high-pitched whine. He planted his feet and waved the hat—and saw them turn and hightail it back at the line of clouds. Shorty felt himself thicken again. And grow, until he stepped out into Big Road and waved the hat at the north wind, and howled like Clint Mixson Moore when he felt the gust die.

At the top of the ladder, Clint Mixson watched the first rig roar over the hill right at Shorty—then the second and third—and felt his heart go hollow. He held his breath, watching Shorty stand his ground and wave the hat, then let the air out in a rush when he saw the rigs slow up and veer around. "I told you so!" he yelled, feeling his heart start to pump blood again. "Didn't I tell you?"

"Tell me what?" Weldon said.

"About old Shorty, and my hat. They handled that convoy all right, between the two of them."

"It was my idea sending that hat down there," Weldon said.

"But my hat."

They pulled the flatbed down to the next intersection and set up again. But the wind was gusting fresh now, the big rigs coming one after the other, and Clint Mixson couldn't make the dead light let go of the bracketplate. He had three nuts off, three bolts in his pocket. But the fourth nut was rusted tight. The corners had rounded off so the wrench kept slipping, and with the rain starting to fall now in fat drops, and the asphalt upreaching, the whole world felt like a lunatic see-saw that the wind kept trying to shake him off of.

At least town traffic was starting to pick up. Methodists and Baptists in their Sunday best leaned out of car windows and hooted at the three of them up on the flatbed, honking and waving to beat all. The carloads of churchgoers meant that the rigs would be done running soon. And all those registered voters driving by seeing that first green light up and shining—and him up on a ladder in the teeth of a Norther, taking down the light that was dead—made Clint Mixson's suffering seem worthwhile.

"Prison for Progress!" Clint Mixson howled, and grinned. "Green means go!"

Shorty felt the rain start to fall. But that crafty old sun was still shining. He set his feet, waved the Stetson at the sun, and saw it duck behind a cloud. Shorty felt his head swell up so there was no way his old hat could hold it. He swept off his broken-brimmed headgear— a tan straw cast-off of Weldon Jackson's, stained with dirt and sweat and oil—and slung it away into the wind. He threw away Clint Mixson Moore's twenty dollars. Then he drew his shoulders back and stepped out into Big Road to face down the line of thunderheads.

Shorty swung the hat over his head and saw the clouds turn into horses. He set his feet and flashed the hat at the sky, seeing the cloudhorses come on. He heard the pound of their hooves, felt the wind from their nostrils, saw the electric flash of their eyes. When another big truck started over the hill, Shorty shifted his stance and waved the hat at the rig, and saw the rig start to slow and veer around. But then he felt the hat shy away out of his hand—spooked, the way a green colt will in just such a wind. He leaped up after it, feeling his hand catch hold of the hat, then feeling his leap lengthen on out across the broad back of the north wind. He felt himself straddle the gale like a cloudmustang he was breaking, there among thunderheads.

Clint Mixson felt cold fingers of breeze take hold of his heart. He saw the hat fly out of Shorty's hand just as the storm broke and the truck started around him. He saw Shorty leap into the path of the oncoming rig. He tried to yell but couldn't find breath. He saw Shorty catch hold of the hat, saw Shorty's head smash against the fender, then saw him pinwheel across the asphalt into the Red Caboose parking lot.

"I can't believe it," Clint Mixson said, finding his breath at last.

"Jesus!" Weldon said. "Come on!"

Clint Mixson followed Weldon down the ladder. Then the two of them jumped off the flatbed and ran hard for the Red Caboose Texaco. "I can't believe it!" Clint Mixson said.

"Shut up and run!"

But Clint Mixson slowed to a walk instead. A crowd was already forming around the spot where Shorty lay, his face gone gray as the hat in the driving rain. Clint Mixson stopped a little distance away from where Weldon knelt over Shorty. People in church clothes knelt also, the wind rippling their umbrellas and whipping up a haze of spray. The truck driver stood with his shoulders hunched, staring down at the dark stain slowly spreading toward the hat that was locked in Shorty's hand.

"I can't believe it," Clint Mixson said.

"Believe it," Weldon said.

Clint Mixson looked back at the dead light dangling aslant from one rusted bolt over the tin roofs of downtown and over the business fronts that were going to stay boarded. He looked at the PRISON

FOR PROGRESS banner as useless now as the old railroad depot. He watched the new traffic light cycle from green to yellow to red. He started walking that way.

"Clint Mixson!" he heard Weldon say, behind him. "What about your hat?"

"Hell," Clint Mixson said, "it's his."

Flight of Doves

We are headed in the direction of the equator now, bouncing northeast in a banana yellow Land Rover across the wrinkled-khaki desert wedge that is western Peru. Straddling the middle of the back bench seat I look forward, through the dust on the windshield, at the foothills of the Andes Mountains rising slowly in front of us out of the sand.

Gray-white, distant, the Andean foothills are as bare, except for gray-green specks of San Pedro cactus and brown puffs of brush, as the hazy blue-white sky is bare of clouds. The dig site is there somewhere. In the Moche Valley, at the base of the foothills, beside a stream flowing down from the mountains. And Thor Heyerdahl waits at the dig site. At least that's what Jack says. Jack ought to know. Jack is going there to see Thor Heyerdahl about a job.

We are far into the back country now. On one more in a long line of rough dirt roads that have been more rough than roads really, hardly roads at all. Just gray-white bands of caliche made from chunks of Andes that have been cut out, crushed, hauled down from among mountains, and stretched long and lean across the khaki sand.

"Not much farther now!" Jack yells. It is Jack's Land Rover doing the bucking, kicking up the dust that soughs in through the open windows with the hot dry air.

"All right, Jack!" David yells.

David's head bounces over the top of the front passenger seat every couple of seconds or so like a black hairy piston. I hear the roar of the engine and of tires on crushed rock, and every now and then a strange, unsettling crunching sound that I pray is not the suspension. Not the suspension, Lord, I pray. Not here in this desert place even You have forsaken, with a broken radio and not much water, short of the foothills and of Thor.

"You sure?" I yell.

"Sure!" Jack yells. "Not much farther now!"

Jack drapes a map across the steering wheel. All wide-open yellow spaces and red, blue, and black letters and lines, it has a tangled look, like the gnarled mass of Jack's hair blowing wild in the blast-furnace breeze. He's had the map out for the last couple of hours or so—it being five hours and more since we pulled out of Jack's big house in Chiclayo, where Jack and David spent most of the night talking about the bayou in Lake Charles that Jack grew up on with David's older brothers and sisters, and I sat re-reading a copy of *Kon-Tiki* that I bought in Lima, studying up on Thor. Looking out at the endless desert on either side of us, the foothills stretching left to right as far as the eye can see, I find myself wishing that I'd studied Jack's map instead.

"Lost" is a word I do not want to think of. This man, I tell myself, is an archaeologist—finding things is his job. This is, after all, the same man who helped set up our trip down the Amazon River, by diesel cargo boat from Yurimaguas on the backside of the Andes down to Iquitos, from Iquitos by steamer to the sea and around the coast to Rio, then by bus through Argentina and Chile, back to Peru. The same man who promised us that if we made it through the Amazon Jungle malaria-free, hepatitis- and cholera-free, he would take us with him to meet Thor Heyerdahl at a working dig site in the desert of northwestern Peru.

The foothills rise so close now I feel as though I could shut my eyes and be among mountains. Forget about the map, I tell myself. Forget about the hours behind us. Give in to the heat and the dry taste of dust and lean back. Brace your feet against the rolling jolts under the wheels and think of cool mountain air and deep blue water. I shut my eyes. I reach out for the foothills I feel so close now, in front of us—and catch hold of a handful of hair.

"Hey!" I hear Jack's voice come from up front. "Hands off!"

I open my eyes and the desert stretches to the horizon on either side. Ahead of us the equatorial sun bleaches the Andes the color of August in Southwest Texas—bone. It is hard to believe that there is water within hours of here, much less a man who sailed halfway across the Pacific on a raft made of balsa logs. *Kon-Tiki*. A raft I sailed through my waking dreams as a boy.

"Is this it?" I hear David say.

"I think this is it," Jack says.

I've heard it twice before. The first time I leaped out of the Land Rover thinking, Thor Heyerdahl! *Kon-Tiki!* A movement of peoples backward and forward across continents, oceans, time. What I got instead was the remains of a dig site long stripped and abandoned, and Jack's stories about grave robbers hiding in the foothills from the police and the army, looting gold and silver and lapis lazuli from the tombs of dead kings and selling the tangible remains of their past at black-market prices. The second time I didn't even bother to climb down into an empty dead end—a dry box canyon where we sat in the banana-yellow convection oven of a Land Rover and listened to another story about how Jack's wife, Anita, a native of these parts who runs a tour agency out of Chiclayo, once got lost out here with the same broken radio, not much water, and a Land Rover full of Belgian tourists. For two days.

"This is it!" I hear Jack say. Again. But this time something in his voice—something half remembered, half imagined, like the mesquite-tree balsa raft of my boyhood dreams—pulls me forward in the seat and carries my thoughts back to Thor. "By God, we've found him."

The hills are gray, with red rock walls that balloon out to encircle the valley. There is brush on both sides of us now, and along the river, trees—scrub oaks, all squat black trunk and dark green leaves, and dusty *algarobas* that look a lot like mesquites, only bigger. Jack eases the Land Rover up under two huge *algarobas* that lean in toward each other to form a giant pool of shade. Behind the trees is a long, lean two-storey skeleton of a building, all raw two-by-fours and concrete foundation, and dark brown men in overalls with straw hats and tools powered by hand. We pile out of the Land Rover almost before it stops, into the sound of hammers and handsaws and the long, smooth scrape of adzes shaping wood.

"Stay here," Jack says. "Don't move. Don't touch anything. Don't even breathe."

"Yes, Jack."

"No problem, Jack."

"And don't call me 'Jack' in front of Thor. From now on it's Doctor Fryeland. Remember that."

Jack stuffs his hair up under a brown safari hat and heads off in search of Heyerdahl, leaving David and me stuck short, standing still. While David does some stretches I lean against the Land Rover, feeling the metal skin burn through my cotton shirt like carried questions. There are so many things I need to know. As many questions as the miles we have covered, as many expectations as people and places seen in a little over three months beneath the equator. Ruins of Inca and Chavin. A bread riot in Cuzco, that the Incas called the Navel of the World. The *coca* leaf grown in the Andes Mountains, in tiny tiered fields with gray rock fences and old Indian men plowing behind mules. The Amazon basin seen from the river, the jungle horizon, the smoke rising from the rain forest on fire in the early evening. Shantytown people working barefoot, loading the fruits of slash-and-burn fields onto boats in the smell of burning. It all runs together like the red-and-blue-and-black letters and lines on Jack's map, pointing us here.

"Does Jack really know Thor Heyerdahl?" I whisper finally, as though Dr. Heyerdahl might overhear.

"What do you mean?" David says.

"I mean, does he really know Dr. Heyerdahl? Or has he only met Dr. Heyerdahl?"

"Jack knows Thor," David drawls, as though he himself has been on a first-name basis with the man for years. "Jack worked a dig with Thor a year or two ago, at a site not far from here."

I wait for David to go on but he stops there, having told me nothing new—leaving me to look elsewhere for answers. Childhood pictures revisited in a breathless pool of shade. Dig sites. Discoveries. A raft of balsa logs cut in the rain forest of Ecuador, roped together in Peru, sailed four thousand three hundred miles across the Pacific Ocean on hope and a theory, to smash ashore on an atoll in Polynesia. A re-enacting of the voyage of a people. A rewriting of textbooks. The account of his adventure, *Kon-Tiki*, titled after the living Sun God of a culture long lost, written with such grace and simplicity as to be read and re-read, dreamed and re-dreamed, by a boy growing up on the Southwest Texas plains.

Then, suddenly, Thor. Gray-haired, blue-eyed, all in khaki and very tall, Dr. Thor Heyerdahl comes bearing down. With the long, loose-jointed strides of a world-walker he comes, throwing out both hands and grinning like a long-lost grandfather.

"Welcome!" he booms. "Welcome to my dig site!"

"Dr. Heyerdahl," Jack says, "this is David Leroy. We come from the same place in Louisiana."

"Hello," David says, and grinning back at Heyerdahl as though he's known him all his life, he pokes a hand into Thor's paw.

"Louisiana!" Heyerdahl booms, pumping hand, arm, shoulder. "The bayou! I once hunted ducks there!"

"That's right!" David booms back. "Lake Charles!"

"And this is," Jack says, "this is . . ."

I feel my face all ablaze as I realize that Jack has forgotten my name. "John," I manage, imagining myself as I must look in Thor Heyerdahl's eyes—pale and sweaty, with a pasty half-grin. "John Hauser. David and I . . . went to the University . . . together."

"The University!" Heyerdahl booms, as his strong hand envelops my hand. "Both of you! That is most excellent! John and David, you must come and see my dig site!"

With those same long, loose-jointed strides that leave us running to stay close, he leads the way up a low rise toward the wooden frame that is being fleshed out into a building. "Our new headquarters!" Heyerdahl shouts. We step over the threshold into the pound of hammers, the chuff of saws, the barked Spanish of Peruvian workmen throwing up walls, fitting rafters, running pipe along the floor. Thor ticks off the high points as we all file by. "Toilet. Kitchen. Dormitory. Private bedroom. Dining room. Office." In between features he gives a running lecture on the merits of hardwood floors versus the expense of buying the best wood. Down the long central hallway, into and out of room after room, I do my best to see a headquarters taking shape—but it remains for me a skeleton, a hollow chest with wooden ribs.

"And now," Thor shouts, "the dig site proper!"

He charges through thickets, across outcrops of rock and clumps of grass dried yellow by the sun. We do our best to keep up with him. My thoughts all awhirl with headquarters half-finished, questions half-formed, hardwood floors, I keep hoping he'll stop for a moment to let me get some kind of handle on the hurricane in my head. I look back and forth between the backs of the men in front of me and the mounds we are climbing toward. But Thor doesn't even slow down.

"We believe all these mounds are buried pyramids!" he shouts. "Part of a religious complex of some kind. But we cannot be sure of anything until the dig progresses."

Six or seven mounds about twenty feet tall surround a central knoll that is much larger. As Heyerdahl leads us toward the hill in the middle, the ground beneath our feet is suddenly full of holes. Some shallow, some as deep as wells, there are more and more of them as we move toward the center, the soil so pockmarked now it looks less like the Peruvian desert than the face of the moon.

"They were dug by looters!" Heyerdahl shouts, as we start around the base of the central knoll. "Looters and grave robbers are a very big problem here in Peru. For some reason, a local legend perhaps, they have concentrated their digging on the western side of this particular complex. This is why we have begun the official dig on the eastern side."

In the eastern shadow of the biggest mound there are no holes. At least, no unofficial ones. Instead the site has been separated out with wooden stakes and twine into squares that are lettered and numbered. The squares have been dug to different depths, all exactly level across the length and width of each grid, each separate depth a different color of earth so that the entire eastern side of the site has a weird kind of 3-D chessboard look. It is here Thor finally stops. He leans back against the dry grass that covers the big central knoll and we gather around him, the late afternoon sun streaming over the shoulders of the buried pyramid like time made visible in the air.

"The different layers are for different civilizations!" Thor booms. "There were at least three here. The Moche, who were a very strong people, a conquering people and good builders, until they forgot their traditions and were weakened and conquered in turn. The Chimu, who conquered the Moche and ruled for a very long time. And the Incas, who dominated the Chimu in their turn. The Incas never invented the wheel and did not have horses, but held sway over half the continent. They did not have writing, but their history went back a thousand years."

"Rememberers," Jack nods, very much Dr. Fryeland now. "Instead of writing things down, the Incas trained men to remember things by reading a pattern of knots tied into strings. They were called Rememberers."

"A great people," Dr. Heyerdahl nods, "conquered in their turn by Western Europeans. Not because they forgot their traditions, but because they remembered them. The Incas remembered white, bearded gods who happened to look very much like Spanish *Conquistadores*. This proved to be very unfortunate for the Incas. But what a civilization! They fitted stones together without mortar and built aqueducts five hundred miles long to carry rainwater to fields. They built cities atop mountains, and desert pyramids."

"Are all these hills really pyramids?" David asks.

"Indeed!" Thor shouts, his voice echoing among the mounds. "Those smaller ones there, and this big one here. This one is mine. They are giving me my own pyramid."

"Giving it to you?" Jack's voice, gone sharp all of a sudden, echoes among the mounds like Thor's. "Who is giving it to you? On what authority?"

"Why, the government of Peru!" Thor shouts. "They have promised to give me this pyramid, and everything in it, for conducting the dig."

"You mean everything uncovered here will belong to you personally?" Jack says.

"Not to me personally, of course. The artifacts will go to the Kon-Tiki Museum in Oslo."

"But," Jack says, "but what about . . ."

Dr. Heyerdahl looks up at Jack with eyes that have seen across oceans. He looks for a long time. Then he gently pats the mound at his side. I see Jack's shoulders slump. I see him turn very slowly and sink down on the khaki-colored earth next to Thor.

"It seems to me a fair bargain all around," Thor says. Then he lowers his voice to what is, for him, almost a whisper. "This will, after all, be a very large and long-term project, spanning many years. With supply problems, being so far from Chiclayo, from any city, and problems with looters and with the rebels in the mountains, it will be a very difficult project to complete. Of course, we will be needing many archaeologists. And the help of reliable people in Chiclayo. Local people, who know the area . . ."

It seems a long time that I stand there watching the two of them, feeling the hurricane of questions in my head slowly fade into a desert sunset breeze. Above us, the stream of light around the shoulders of the mound deepens, turns to gold, before Thor realizes that David and I are still there.

"Run along, boys!" he says, looking up at us with eyes that have spent a lifetime answering questions. "If you run very fast, and climb very hard, you can catch the sunset from the top of the cliff."

As suddenly as that David and I are headed uphill, sprinting across uneven ground toward the top of the valley. A spine of rock angles up eastward toward the Andes that have gone red now in the light of the dying day. Racing the sun and each other over the stones that slip, the brush that cuts, we top out finally and stand, our breath coming heavy, with the Andes Mountains at our backs. Before us, the red globe of the sun dives toward the desert across the valley below.

I open my eyes wide, feeling the sunset burn into my memory like boyhood sunsets in the branches of my mesquite-tree balsa raft, when I stared into the sinking sun until I thought I'd go blind. I see mounds below us all around the spine of rock. Ancient lookouts must have climbed this same spur of hills and looked out over this same valley into the desert. Moche lookouts, watching for the Chimu who would come to conquer them. Chimu lookouts, watching for the Incas. Inca lookouts, watching for the Spaniards who would conquer them in turn. From this height the mounds look regular, laid out in a pattern of squares. Underneath the mounds are buildings. Bones. Tangible remains of the past, waiting to be dug up and carried away.

On the far side of the mounds I see the ground fall away toward the river and the skeleton that will be the diggers' quarters. I make out workmen, tiny in the distance, their tools flashing in the fading light. The tool sound drifts faintly up the valley. With the noise comes smoke—as though the sun, sinking now into the floor of the desert, has set the world on fire. Out of the blaze I see a bird come flying up the valley, dark gray and moving fast. A dove. Then more, and yet more. I realize, as the birds come thicker and thicker, that it isn't smoke I see in the air, but thousands of doves.

Some carry over the wall we stand on. Others peel off to settle into the scrub oaks and *algarobas* along the river, or into nooks of shadow in the red rock walls. I find myself looking around for a mesquite tree, but there are no mesquites here to settle into. No balsa rafts. No roar of Pacific waves. I watch the last few doves fly out of the sun that has faded now like my questions to a pinpoint, a drop of blood.

I can barely make out Jack and Thor. They lean in deepening shadow against the side of the big pyramid. Thor's pyramid. Two khaki spots against the sunset-colored earth. An old man and a young man among mounded shadows, whispering about digging up bones.

Andrew Geyer is so skillful with imagery that you will see the places he describes, be they grain fields in Texas or boats along the Amazon River. You will love this collection of finely-crafted stories.

JERRY CRAVEN

Geyer sings a new and engaging kind of Texas blues. Funny and compassionate, wacky and smart, the stories here mark a fine debut.

JAMES HOGGARD

Whispers in Dust and Bone *conveys the gritty reality of life in Texas. Whether they cling to their lives in the Lone Star state or attempt to escape it by traveling south of the border, the characters seek a safe place. While the rugged landscape has taught them that emotion is an open door welcoming trouble, these characters want desperately to feel sorrow and loss, joy and comfort. Harsh and stubborn, his women struggle to love; though worn by the climate, his men find themselves succumbing to moments of tenderness. This is a fine first collection.*

JILL PATTERSON

Geyer's tales are subtly layered, infused with biblical allusion, history, philosophy, myth, and the harsh, unforgiving ambience of the author's native Southwest Texas. His characters, rugged as the landscape that shapes them, emerge before the reader full-blown, fashioned from the clay of the actual, tooled by uncertainty, courage, triumph, tragedy and the unpredictable turns of human love. This is a seamless, remarkable collection of stories by a writer comfortable with place, knowledgeable in the universal yearnings of the human heart.

LARRY D. THOMAS